Karen the Origin Story

Author: Andre Johnson

Contributions By: Roy F.

Daniel U.

Authors other books on Amazon:

Tedzells Poems and Short Stories

Discount Code: books

10% Off Order

https://www.etsy.com/shop/Tedzells

In the antebellum era 1812-1861 "Miss Ann" was used. As late as 2018, before the use of "Karen" caught on. Alternate names used before Karen such as Barbecue Becky and Permit Patty.

 Example of phrase: *His mama washes clothes on Wednesday for Miss Ann. Karen called the police on people hanging out at the park.*

Table of Content:

Chapter 1

The weather was nice. A cool breeze swept over the plains, as the tall grasses swayed in unison. The sun was decent, hiding behind the clouds, the perfect position for a picnic under the apple trees. That was Anita's thought as she carried her basket towards the maize farm. The stalks had grown mighty tall over the summer. Heads of maize rounded the stalks, their tuffs falling out like flowery waterfalls. She saw her aunt in the distance, hunching over a stalk as she twisted the ripe cobs from the stalk. "The weather looks nice today," she chirped, voicing out her earlier thought. Aunt Rachel looked up. her squint morphing into a small smile. Her tiny glasses sat atop her nose. stained with small specks of sand and her white head covering had pushed back a little showing her hair. Aunt Rachel adjusted her cap to the front. "You are correct, my dear. Bless the Lord for this fine weather," she said and shifted her focus to the stalks. Aunt Rachel's cap had seen better days. Anita thought it was odd, Aunt Rachel had only two.

Anita knew their community emphasized on minute spending, but she didn't think five caps would be too much. That was the amount she possessed. Sighing. she dropped her basket and set to work. pushing through maize stalks picking out ripe cobs. She wanted minimal stains on her dress, so she'd worn an apron over it. Her dress was a plain blue one, reaching to her ankles and forming a pleat at her waist. The sleeves were long and puffed at the shoulder area, following the recommended style for girls her age at the community. Unlike hers, Aunt Rachel's dress was black signifying that she was a married woman. Another part of the rules. She didn't know who made them. she just knew it had been passed down from generation to generation. This was the type of tradition that kept the community together. It was good for them and she had grown up with those traditions so close to her heart.

As much as she tried to prevent it, sand still entered her shoes. They were blocky with a silver buckle. It should have protected her. Soon as she could feel the grains pinch the sole of her feet it became uncomfortable. She wiped the sweat from her forehead and was about to take them off when she saw Noah. Noah, her twin who was approaching them. His footsteps crunched through the sand as he squinted at them, a hand on his waist. The other hand held a pitch fork, swung over his shoulder. "Can we take a break, Aunt?" He stopped just in front of them and crouched. "Not yet, my dear," she replied. Noah black felt hat covered half of his face and his suspender trousers were stained with grit from the soil as well. When he looked up, his eyes meeting Anita's, she couldn't help but marvel at the similarities they both possessed.

Of course, she should've expected it; they were both twins, so they were bound to share similarities. But it didn't seize to fascinate her. Another one of God's wonders for her to think over. Their eyes were the same shade of light green with golden specks swimming in the iris. It bore the same spark of curiosity they'd held ever since they were children. Only that they were curious about different things. Their lips were thin and slanted upwards as if in a permanent small smile and freckles dotted the bridges of their nose. Their hair, golden brown was always hidden under the white cap and black hat respectfully. They also had the same height. Tall enough to reach the topmost shelf in the kitchen when no one else could.

Despite all these similarities, there were also the differences that shaped them into their own persons. While their eyes both held curiosity. Anita's were soft with natural wonder, a kind that sought to appreciate and marvel at things she came across. Noah's were steeled with an explorer's determination. He sought to delve deep into the complexities of those things and discover as much as he could. Puberty had contributed much to shaping them. Anita was rounder around the edges, forming curves where they needed to be with a supple flesh. Noah's frame was firm with lean muscles and a hardened jaw. He was frequently complaining of how much hair he had to shave off every morning. Unmarried men were forbidden from having facial hair.

He was still crouched on the ground. Anita didn't say a word to him. More like there was nothing to say. Unlike him, she didn't have the luxury of resting. She was sure Aunt Rachel would throw a tantrum if she decided to stop too. Aunt would say they were piling all the work on her. So, one person resting was enough. Soon, as the sun shifted in its position overhead and hours passed, her basket was full of maize cobs. Anita heaved a sigh and wiped the sweat from her forehead. Noah was asleep on the ground, his hat covering his face. "Alright, let's move, my loves," Aunt Rachel finally said. Anita released a breath she'd held. If Aunt Rachel had said they should go for another hour again, she would faint. Already, her bones groaned from straining them so much and a hot bath was the only thing on her mind at the moment. "Wake up." She lightly kicked Noah by his torso. He groaned and stretched. "Are we finished?" Anita rolled her eyes at the statement. Like you did anything. Aunt Rachel was ahead of them on the path. Anita slowed her steps to meet Noah behind. It was a normal routine. This was the only time they were both alone. They were always surrounded by aunts, uncles, cousins, church members, or their friends, Lizzy and Jedidiah. They took any chance they got to speak with each other. Some of the things they said had to be said in secret anyway. They did break a lot of rules, much to Anita's guilt and Noah's excitement.

"You slept all through," she declared almost in an accusatory tone. "Hey, I was working too. I just closed my eyes and whoosh." He threw his hands in the air. "I got carried away and slept off." She shook her head and adjusted the basket under her arms. "Well, you know what's going to happen soon. I've been listening in on Uncle's conversation with the preacher. They would announce the Rumspringa soon for us." This took Noah by surprise. He slowed to a stop, mouth open. "Come on," she whispered and grabbed his arm, pulling him along. "She's going to be suspicious." Honestly, Anita didn't understand why he was so surprised. It was a normal custom in the Amish society. They were not yet baptized into the religion as fully fledged members. When they turned sixteen, they would be 'let loose'. They had the opportunity to leave the community into the modern world and explore everything there was to explore. Shopping malls, parties, alcohol…

The thought thrilled her and scared her at the same time. All her life she had lived in the confines of the community, cut off from the world beyond. They never used electricity or phones. She's heard so many interesting stories about the outside world. Stories that were said in a whisper, away from the ears of others. They did fascinate her. she couldn't help the guilt that ate at her heart as she marveled over them. Now, they were releasing her into that same world. It would definitely be unusual adventure. After exploring the modern world, they would have to come to a decision. They would either choose to stay in that world or come back and be baptized as a member, swearing to follow all Amish beliefs. She was fascinated by the modern world, but she loved her community as well. A silence had settled between them. She looked beside her. Noah's eyes were brimming with excitement. She didn't expect less. "I wasn't expecting it to be so soon," he said.

"Me neither."

"We should tell Lizzy and Jedidiah," he said.

"Yes, let's tell them."

The four of them usually met in the secret of the night after dinner. They had picked an abandoned old shed far away from their houses to meet. It wasn't that meeting was wrong. it was what they were meeting to talk about. Why it had to be a secret. what they were doing and what they were hiding. Specifically, Noah's stuff. The hours passed. They had Anita helped Aunt Rachel to cook the dinner with her other two daughters while the twin girls set the table. Their Aunt had given birth to seven children. Adding Noah and Anita made it nine people they had to feed every day. It was pretty normal to have that many children. Anita thought she would have been in the same situation too, having many siblings. But, after her mother gave birth to Noah and her she died to complication.

The twin's father died of a heart attack last year their life was never the same. they were officially orphans. They had no mother or father to call her own and there was a constant emptiness in their chest. Noah acted like he was ok, but she knew deep down, he was still healing from the loss. Imagine, Aunt Rachel and Uncle David taking care of an extra seven children. It would be chaotic for sure. Soon, the food was ready. She served the cornmeal in bowls and cut up large squares of bread in small flat plates. The dining table was soon set and filled up by the whole family. Uncle David and his first son both sat at the heads of the table. The only thing lighting up the dining room was a gas lamp, hanging in the corner. Once they were set, Uncle David declared. "Let us pray."

All heads bowed in unison and they listened as he prayed. Once he was done, a simultaneous 'amen' left the lips of everybody. They ate in total silence like they always did. The sound of their cutleries and plates disturbing the night's silence. Once they had finished eating the women cleared the table. Then Anita took her blanket and stepped out into the night, meeting Noah who was waiting for her. Though the shed was tucked away from plain sight, it wasn't that far. Soon they'd reached the shed. Noah brought out a key and opened the lock, pulling the wooden bar across the door, aside. It was dark inside. She watched Noah's frame search the walls with his hands. There was a click and immediately, the place was flooded with light. The shed had a space in the middle with stacks of hay piled in four places: their makeshift chairs. But it was what surrounded them. Anita's heart was racing.

Scraps of metal, wires, damaged devices from the outside world, tools, books on science and technology, literature and every other thingamabob that should not be within the Amish community. All of them, a product of Noah's tinkering. She usually frowned at it, nagging his ear off. But when he'd introduced her those novels, she couldn't help herself. And she had to admit, it was interesting seeing Noah invent strange things. The science books were also fascinating. A world beyond the farming and textile she was involved in. Soon, Lizzy and Jedidiah arrived cloaked with their blankets. Lizzy was a red head with a gap tooth, sparkling blue eyes and a charming smile. Anita was sure she had a crush on Noah. Jedidiah was not much different from Noah. His hair was blond, cropped at the edges and he was just as tall as Noah. Only thing was, he had a slight hunch. "Welcome everybody. Let's start the meeting," Noah said.

Chapter Two

Noah faced the trio, their face rife with expectation. He grinned and then said, "I have news." Then he paused for effect, letting his revelation settle in their minds. He liked to hold the attention of the people he spoke to, just enough to brew their curiosity. He saw Anita rolled her eyes. A smirk appeared on his face and he cleared his throat. "They're going to release us for the Rumspringa soon," he announced. Noah watched the expression on their faces. Anita's bland look, Jedidiah's stunned look and Lizzy's beaming face. Lizzy was the first to speak. "Really? Wow. That was so fast. Why are they releasing us so early?" she asked. I'm personally not so sure about that. It must be because of the wedding coming up soon. Preacher Mark wants to send us off as soon as possible and be rid of us. Noah deduced. "Hm. I think you're right." Jedidiah said. He placed his finger under his chin as a habit and made circles, in deep thought.

"Anyways." Anita slapped her hands and adjusted on the seat, "We have a lot of planning to do. Where do we go? Where are we going to stay? Do you want to actually go?" Noah found the question ridiculous. Of course, he wanted to go. The only opportunity to go and explore the world was right at his feet. Why would he want to stay back? He scoffed and waved his hand dismissively. "Of course, I'm going. You can stay back if you want to," he said. Anita scowled. "That's not the point I'm making. Besides, you're not the only one here. Also, my point is what our plan is for the Rumspringa. Are we really going to… try all those things?" She looked at them one by one, her expression betraying her feelings.

Noah almost let out a sigh. Anita was the one who always hid in a shell. Right from when they were little, he didn't think if any other person who was as careful as an earthworm in a salt mine. It slowed him down sometimes. But when he thought about it more, he concluded that it was good for them. He knew how impulsive he could be, jumping into things without caution. But she kept him in check most times and it helped him avoid horrible circumstances. He too made her more aware of the world and heightened her curiosity as he pulled her along on his adventures. "Well, I want to go," Lizzy said in a small voice, tucking her head between her thighs. "I don't believe that we're going to go off the cliff doing the most horrible things, but we could get to experience so many things. Like electricity… and television. It would be fun."

Noah smiled at the submission. Lizzy was what people thought Anita was. Even with her silent aura, Lizzy was just as curious as he was. Though not as active, but her curiosity was there. Anita was the one in a shell. She needed to be pulled out all the time. Jedidiah nodded his head in agreement. Noah thought back to when they'd become friends. He had just transferred to this Amish community from his own community after his parents died. Fairly new and all, he went to watch a game of softball at the field. There was a small argument going on behind about the bases. Interested, he eavesdropped on the conversation. But at the end, they dismissed it and declared that it didn't matter. It reminded him of the days at his community where they looked at him as if he was mad, the way he raved on and on about science and all it had to offer.

As the boys behind him came to a conclusion. Jedidiah suddenly said, "I do really wonder what's up there though." That was enough for him. Someone else was as curious as he was. Someone else shared the same wonder he did. So, he approached him after the game and the rest is history. Anita had found Lizzy in the fields one time looking for butterflies. Lizzy looked for butterflies and took note of them, drawing them, differentiating their physical characteristics and giving them their own names. She had a large leather-bound book of different animal species she had studied. A scientist in his own right. Anita introduced her and the rest too was history. Soon, he found the abandoned shed, started building things from the aid of the science books he collected from the doctors office just outside town. He was skeptical at first but thought it right to show his friends the shed. Fast forward to today and they were together planning the Rumspringa. Noah snapped out from his thoughts. Anita had a look of guilt on her face. He immediately felt a pang of shame. She was just airing her fears. "Anita, do you not want to go?"

"I do," she's said.

"So, what is the problem?" Lizzy said, placing a palm on her shoulder.

"I'm just nervous. This is a completely new experience," she said.

"You don't have to be. We'll be together," Jedidiah suddenly said.

Noah's brows shot into his forehead. "Together?" he voiced his thought.

"Yeah. Well…" Jedidiah adjusted and leaned forward. This made everybody follow suit. When you talked about the Rumspringa, I was thinking. My maternal aunt is a landlady in the city side. My parents can arrange for her to let us have two rooms. Noah and I would stay in the first. And Anita and Lizzy would stay in the second. There was silence for some seconds, each person digesting the new information. "Are you sure she's going to agree to that?" Anita spoke. "Definitely. But we are going to pay a little money for the time we spend there. That's not a problem, is it? We can do it," Jedidiah said. "I love the plan!" Lizzy said all bubbly and excited. She ended the sentence with a laugh.

Noah stood, hands on his hips with a smile. And Anita beamed. Things were going in motion. He loved the friends he had. For that night, they'd agreed on where they were going to stay. They would inform their parents about the arrangement once the Rumspringa was announced for them. Noah was sure none of their guardians would object. The four of them were tight at the hip, so that it was no surprise they'd be going together. A week passed and true to Anita's words, they were called to the sitting room to be prayed for and send into the world. They had packed their luggage filled with supplies and food items by Aunt Rachel. By the time they were supposed to leave, Aunt Rachel was in tears and Uncle Ben had a solemn look across his face.

His other cousins lined up to say their goodbyes. He couldn't help the sadness that had grown in his chest. No matter how exciting Rumspringa sounded like, he was aware of the gravity of the period. For every family releasing their ward, there was a possibility the child would come back and declare that he no longer wants to be part of the Amish community. He understood the weight bearing on their hearts, but on the other hand, the world beyond called to his soul. Soon, a truck pulled up in front of the house. Lizzy and Jedidiah were already inside, their bags was also. While Anita stayed at the front, he squeezed himself behind with the others. Learning to drive was something he was going to try to achieve. They were not allowed to own cars, but they could let someone drive them. Noah wasn't sure what exactly he was going to do in the city, but there were a lot of endless possibilities to explore from.

They waved their goodbyes and soon the truck was on the move. The drive was silent throughout, each with their own thoughts. They passed bushes and fields for an hour. The houses became bigger and they increased in number as they advanced towards the city. It was obvious once they'd crossed the farm side into the major parts of the city. The cars zoomed past them without restrictions. The English, a name they called non-

Amish people, were of different types milling about like chickens in a coop. The noise was thunderous compared to the quiet of the farm side. The buildings became taller and bigger, some holding neon-colored signs, some flashing their wares through see through windows. The air here was thicker compared to the cleaner air at the farm side. Noah didn't know about the others, but the blood under his skin zipped around from excitement. He pressed his face against the window, making surprised sound and sounds of awe sometimes. The driver kept giving him worried glances. Noah didn't care. He would absorb every single thing he could.

Soon they left the much busier streets and entered a more controlled area dotted with apartments and houses with beautiful yard gardens outside. The truck stopped at a six-storied apartment block with balconies looking out on the main street. They took out their bags and paid the truck driver. "Jed. This is the place, right?" Anita said, inspecting the building. It was a pale-yellow color with paint peeling off from the edges. The metal railings had rusted and when the wind came strong, it rattled. Jedidiah took out a paper, looked at it and then looked at the building. "Yeah, I think so. It says number thirteen," he said and pointed to the sign by the side. "My aunt lives on the ground floor. Room 2."

"Alright then, lead the way," Noah said.

They entered into a dimly lit corridor. The light flickered as they marched through the ground floor to the very end of the corridor. The doors had number markings engraved on them. Jedidiah stopped in front of the number two and then knocked. They waited with hushed breaths. In some seconds the door clicked and it creaked open. Noah didn't know what to expect but the woman in front of him didn't fit image in his head. Her face looked like it had a permanent scowl etched on and her skin was wizened, dry and cracked. Her hair hung disgracefully over her head in scattered tufts and when her lips parted, her teeth were yellow. Her eyes looked sunken and when they pinned on him, a shiver ran down his spine. She grunted and disappeared back inside. They all stood there, stunned. Well, except Jedidiah. He had a normal expression on.

She returned with two keys. "Take room seven and eight on the third floor." She slapped the keys into Jedidiah's palms. "No messing up the place. I kick you out if you turn my rooms into a mess. And remember, I'm getting my dues at the end of the month." Jedidiah smiled. "Thank you, Aunt Shel." The door slammed in our faces. There was silence. "Well, that was… interesting," Anita chuckled and laughed dryly. "Let's go," Jedidiah said, leading the way.

They didn't have a lot of possessions, so carrying out luggage up the stairs wasn't so grueling. They found their rooms. Jedidiah gave the girls their key and opened the boys' room. The room was a pretty square space with nothing but a bunk bed, a desk and a closet at the other end. There were two door, one leading to a kitchen and the other to the toilet. The space was bland, painted in a bland yellow color and the bunk beds were decked with bare mattresses. But it was still workable. They would be spending some months in this space, but they would find their way around it. Hopefully. They went to work, fixing the mattresses, dusting off the windows, sweeping and mopping the dust-layered floor. Then they finally felt comfortable to start unpacking their bags.

Chapter Three

Noah had just out up the last of his suspenders in the closet. It was oddly satisfying the saw his set aligned with Jedidiah's. They almost had the same set of clothing and they could wear each other's clothes without even knowing. Jedidiah had joked about it and they had laughed at the thought of switching clothes. But now, it was time for business. Noah went to the girls' room beside them, and knocked in the door, alerting them to a meeting. Soon, the girls joined them in their room. As a form of courtesy, they let the girls sit on the bottom bunk and Jedidiah sat on the top while Noah faced them to address them. "We've finally reached the city," he declared with an air of magic as he threw his hands in the air and smiled.

Jedidiah whooped. Anita smiled and Lizzy clapped. "Thank you, thank you," Noah bowed. "Now on to the topic of the day. Jedidiah helped us with getting a place to stay for a small price. Round of applause for Jedidiah please," he motioned towards them. The trio clapped as Jedidiah beamed and tipped his hat. "Alright, the question remains, what are we going to do while we are here? What are the plans we have? Personally, I do not have any plans yet. I want to explore a lot of things, but they are all scattered in my head, so it's not clear yet.

Anita." She snapped her head in his direction. "Do you have any plans?" he said.

She pursed her lips and looked towards the window. "Well, it's not much, but I want to visit a classy restaurant and see how it is. I've heard a lot about those." "Hmm, interesting." Noah mused and walked over to the desk, pulling out a sheet of paper and grabbing a pencil. He wrote in capital letters, "MAPPED OUT PLAN OF THINGS WE WANT TO DO." Underneath, he wrote: Number 1. Go to a classy restaurant. "What about you Lizzy?" he said. "I'm not so sure for now. I must think carefully about it," she said. "Okay, Jedidiah?" he faced Jedidiah. "I want to go to an internet café. My brother told me about those when he visited," Jedidiah said.

Everybody avoided the topic of his elder brother as much as possible. Abandoning the community after his Rumspringa made the community duller. His presence was refreshing and he was an all-round good guy. Everybody loved him. Nobody expected he would leave the faith so easily, but the cold reality came creeping on them. He declared that he loved the outside world and would find purpose there. Naturally, he was cut off and people barely spoke about him. So, hearing Jedidiah reference his brother was a breath of fresh air. Noah was sure it sparked memories in the minds of all of them. He wrote again: Number 2: Go to an internet café.

There was an old clock hanging on the wall that seemed to be working well. It was just one o'clock in the afternoon. "What do you suggest we do first?" he said. Lizzy spoke. "We can do both of them today, I believe. Going to a restaurant and internet café is not that time consuming, I presume." "Yes," Anita replied. "It will also give us the opportunity to scout the place and find out where the important places are." "How much do we have in total?" Jedidiah asked. Noah mentioned the price. The Amish rarely spent a lot of money on groceries and important things, so it was going to cover them for a month at least. Considering if they don't spend stupidly. Noah closed the meeting. They decided they would meet downstairs after ten minutes. It would give them time to freshen up. There was no difference really. All the shirts looked the same. So, he took the one he thought looked the cleanest, buttoned it to the last button on his neck, tucked it into his black suspender pants and placed his black hat on his head. It was exactly the same as Jedidiah. Just like everyone at the community, most of the males dressed the same.

They put on their shoes and headed downstairs, waiting for the ladies. Soon, they had arrived. There was not much difference. They had their hair tucked into the white cap and they wore their ankle-length dresses. His sister's dress was a dull yellow and Lizzy's was blue. Anita carried a satchel where all the money was and when they had confirmed they were ready, they set off moving to nowhere in particular. The environment was a very different experience to the group. Their heads swung every which way as they passed the buildings lining the sides of the roads. Occasionally, a few cars would zoom past them. It was a mostly quiet neighborhood away from the hustle and bustle of the center of the city. Noah was grateful for that at least. There was still some semblance of the farm side around the city. He was excited, but he didn't know how he would have handled it if he was surrounded by so much noise.

They'd gone on for about thirty minutes when Anita suddenly spoke. "Lizzy, Noah, Jedidiah, I think we should stop and ask for directions. We obviously don't know where we are going." Noah quickly agreed. "You're right. At this rate, we are going to find ourselves in another part of the world." "Let's keep going then. When we come across somebody, we will ask," Lizzy said. But it was really a funny situation. because as they advanced, the people on the streets increased. Here was their chance to ask for directions, but none of them made a move. The reason was evident even to the blind. It was those looks. The looks they received were…Noah tried to find the word to qualify them. Was it disgust? Confusion? Their eyes held the expressions that screamed volumes. Like they wanted to be far away from them. Noah felt like a spectacle as they drew pairs of eyes from all directions. Their gazes burned holes on their backs, but they still moved ahead. He could hear the laughter directed at them, he could see the judgement in their eyes, throwing daggers at them.

Deep down, they knew the reason why, but no one was willing to speak. Not just yet. So, what if they dressed differently? What if they lived life differently? They wee just different. He didn't see any Amish people throwing slurs in the way of the Englishers because of their lifestyle. So why all the bile? As they advanced, he could feel the taste in his mouth sour. His heart twisted in a chest and a frown settled on his forehead. The expressions on the face of the others mirrored him. Jedidiah stepped forward. "We've been moving for far too long. I'm going to ask for direction." Noah admired his bravery. The way these people looked at them like they were unwanted pests, he wasn't sure if he would be able to hold his tongue. They passed a few more people, ignoring their stares and when they came across a group of guys all standing on a corner. All occupied with each other so Jedidiah took this opportunity to approach them. The rest followed.

"Hello," he said.

The group paused their conversation and turned to them. Immediately, their expressions morphed into astonishment. The one at the front, closest to them, let his eyes roam them from head to toe, his wonder deepening. Jedidiah cleared his throat. "Could I get directions to the nearest restaurant please?" "Yoooo! What are you guys wearing?" One said and the others started to laugh. Noah felt heat travel through his cheeks and then his forehead. He bit his tongue, trusting Jedidiah to handle the situation. "It's the twenty-first century bro. y'all be dressing like Queen Elizabeth's minions." Another came forward and tipped Jedidiah's hat. The rest burst into laughter as if it was even funny in the first place.

Noah formed fists by his side. He could feel his blood thrum under his veins with anger. And he wasn't usually this angry. He'd not been angry in a long time. These people were bullying them just because of their different dressing? Jedidiah steadied his hat on his head. Noah had to give it to him, the guy had self-control. "I'm sorry. I just need directions to a restaurant around," he stated. The smile wiped off that one guy's face. He stepped an inch closer to Jedidiah, menacingly. "Oh yeah? If you wanna get a reply, you better drop that tone of yours." What tone?! He'd asked the question without any hidden motive. Noah gritted his teeth. Anita stepped forward in his line of vision. He grabbed her arm and pulled her back, sending her a warning look.

Suddenly a voice came from the back. "Stop." The guys cleared to form a path and a much older man walked through. He had a cigarette stuck in his lips. It was the first time he was seeing a cigarette up close. The smoke wafted through Noah's nose and he coughed. The man's eyes shifted to Noah studied him, then to Lizzy, Anita and then back to Jedidiah. "You new in this town?" he said. Jedidiah nodded. "Good. Take a look at these faces. This is our territory. We run this place and we can fuck shit up anytime. Understood?" Jedidiah nodded again. The man gave a single nod and took one long drag of his cigarette and puffed it into the air. Lizzy coughed this time. "Y'all Catholics or som'n?" he asked. "We're Amish," Jedidiah said. "Hmm." He nodded. "I know them Amish folks. They're cool to me." Then he turned to face Jedidiah squarely. "There's a restaurant close by. If you walk to the end of the road, there is a bank, turn the corner and you will see a restaurant."

"Thank you," Jedidiah smiled.

The man grunted. "Just make sure you watch your back on these streets." Jedidiah tipped his hat and led them away. When they were finally out of earshot, Noah burst into an angry tirade. He talked of how condescending they were and how they acted like they owned the whole world. He told them how much he had tried to hold himself back. Anita said she would have whacked them with her satchel. Lizzy said she would give them a whooping. Jedidiah on the other hand, told them he'd been expecting something like that to happen. His elder brother had told him all about his experience so he had knowledge to equip him. Nothing was going to take him by surprise apparently.

True to the man's words, they reached the restaurant around the corner of the bank. It was at an intersection with white lines across the streets. Jedidiah had told them it was for people without cars. He also told them how the traffic lights worked. So, when it turned red, the cars would stop and they would cross the street. So, they waited for the light to turn red and then they crossed. They murmured to each other what a brilliant idea it was, especially in such a busy place like this. The restaurant had neon lights flashing at the top of the building. Where there should've been walls, it was just tall windows giving passerby's a view of the inside. It was awkward at first as they pushed the glass door open and huddled inside the restaurant, gathering at the corner.

The temperature was unusually colder compared to the normal warm weather. Noah rubbed his arms, looking around. Then, he spotted the AC's, like the one he saw in his books. As expected, a silence settled in the restaurant. Noah didn't have the time to marvel at the structure and architecture of the place. The eyes of everybody were pinned on them. Enough to make him uneasy. A lady in a uniformed apron approached them. "Can you leave the restaurant please?

Chapter Four

Anita was stunned. She couldn't understand why they were being asked to leave. This time it was her turn to speak. She clamped her lips together and stepped forward, facing the waiter. "For what reason are you asking us to leave?" she asked. The waiter looked confused for a moment. She looked at them one by one and then slowly said, "Are you here to eat?" Anita drew her head back from the absurdity of the question. What else would they be there to do? Was there a place in her mind where she'd mixed up what a restaurant was supposed to be for? "Of course, we are here to eat. Or do you not serve food to customers?" she said through gritted teeth.

The waiter blinked again. In the silence of the restaurant, the only sound Anita could hear was the whirring of a machine somewhere in the back. Just like before when she had been walking down the street, she felt like a spectacle. An interesting shiny thing to be watched and studied. An odd thing. "Um… sorry, give me a minute." The waiter said and disappeared behind the counter. Anita released a breath she'd been holding as her chest deflated. She placed both hands on her hips and looked at her friends. They didn't say it, but they could see the hope in their eyes dwindling to nothing. They went on this journey with a lot of expectations to be able to explore and find out more about the world. It was proving difficult. They were just hours in on their first day and they'd already encountered a lot of problems because of their identity. It made her feel like they didn't belong. Like they weren't supposed to be there.

There were hushed sounds coming from the counter side. The waiter was discussing with someone in hushed tones and they threw covert glances at the group. Anita's patience was growing thin. The air around then had grown thick with tension. They were all tense. It was because she wanted to experience a restaurant that they were all being embarrassed. The ambience was nice. Bulbs emitting cool yellow light hung from straight rods. The walls were covered with colorful wallpapers. The round wooden tables were surrounded by petite round chairs and a soft music played from the speakers. The place looked welcoming enough for them to have a wonderful experience. So why were they being barred from that?

A chair screeching on the floor drew the attention of the people. A tall blond lady with sunglasses hanging on the neck of her shirt waltzed over with a coy smile on her lips. Anita unconsciously stepped back in line with the rest of the group. "Hi, you're really making us uncomfortable. Can you leave?" the lady batted eyelashes that were unusually long and plastered a fake smile of her oily lips. "In what way are we making you uncomfortable?" Noah spoke. His voice boomed against the walls of the restaurant. He'd not spoken a word since the ordeal on the streets and she was sure he had been holding back a lot of anger. "I mean," the lady looked around and then back at us. "You guys look so weird. Are you even part of human civilization? It's giving me the creeps. I don't know who you guys are but it doesn't seem like you fit in this place."

To say she was surprised would be an understatement. She was flabbergasted. It was a word she'd learnt in one of the literature books. Her mouth dropped open. She heard Lizzy gasp beside her. "How rude?" Anita said. "We belong here as much as anybody does. You are not in any position to tell us what to do" Her speech was interrupted by a cold liquid spreading from the top of her dress and soaking it through. Instantly, the restaurant erupted. There were gasps and shouts ringing through the place, ringing through her head. She stared dumbfounded at the red liquid that'd formed a map on her chest. Her eyes almost bulged out of the sockets and her blood froze under her skin. Lizzy grabbed her arm, looking between them like she couldn't believe her eyes.

She stared at the stain and then at the lady. "Oops. At least you get to change that hideous thing you call a dress." Anita couldn't believe it. The sheer wickedness. How could someone do this to her? She did nothing to deserve this. She only stood her ground and declared that she belonged. Tears burned at the back of her eyes. She blinked them away, fighting against the tightness of her throat. Jedidiah threw his arm over her neck and muttered words her brain couldn't recognize. He was trying to soothe her, but it wasn't working. In a flash, from her line of vision, Noah stomped forward towards the counter. For some reason, she suddenly forgot her predicament. She knew how explosive Noah could be. There was no telling what he would do. Anita slapped a hand over her mouth as a gasp left her lips.

Noah stopped in front of the counter, glared at them and then swiped the towel hanging on a bar. He stomped back and handed it to Anita. "Let's go," he said with an edge to his voice and without a word, everybody followed. The walk back was silent. They were downcast and tired from the insults they'd received there. Anita felt hot-anger brew in her chest. There was no word to explain this kind of anger. It was the type that consumed her from the inside. Every cell in her body itched for revenge. Jedidiah broke the silence. "Cheer up, everyone. This is just one bad experience. We still have the internet café to go to. My brother said"

"No one cares what your brother said right now." Noah snapped. A chill settled in the air. They all froze on the spot, Noah included. He groaned and ran a palm down his face. "I'm very sorry, Jed. I was just very angry. I should bridle my tongue like Preacher Mark says." Jedidiah nodded. "I understand. We're all human. But I won't lie to you and say your words did not hurt me." "I know. Forgive me," Noah sighed and shifted his gaze. Going on this Rumspringa was probably a bad idea. They were already having internal issues on their first day. This rarely happened to them. Lizzy butted in. "Let's go to the internet café. Jedidiah is right. This is just one experience. Were we expecting it to be all rosy? No, right? Come on, let's go." Yes, I was expecting it to be rosy, she thought. Like before, they attracted stares from people. Some even brought out those things called phones and started taking pictures of them. But, unlike the first time, this was different. They marched with a determination that steeled their bones and affirmed their identity. They weren't going to cower in front of anybody because of who they were.

They asked an old lady for directions to an internet café. Her warm smile and manner of approach thawed the ice in their hearts. When they found the café, it was safe to say, they were springy again. Inside, the number of computers lying in rows was mind blowing. The screens blinked at them with different characters and graphics as people sat in front of these computers, going through different variety of things. The found two spaces free. Jedidiah sat in the first seat and Anita sat in the second. She stared at the screen, studying the little boxes that lined the screen on the left side and a landscape picture filling the rest of the screen. Jedidiah muttered, "I just need to find a 'google'"

"What's that?" Lizzy said. Noah was the one that answered. "I hear it is a thing that searching for anything on the internet. Like a song or any question, you ask." Jedidiah nodded. "You're right. My brother told me about it—Oh, I've found it." He grabbed the oval pod thing he called a mouse and as he moved it, the arrow moved. He tapped on the google icon and it opened into another screen. "My brother says I should search an artist called Anya," Jedidiah said. "Artist as in singer? You want to play a song?" Anita said. Music is forbidden if it comes from technology in their community, so she couldn't help the guilt that began to grow. She adjusted the towel on her chest. She'd used it to cover the stain. She was already odd enough in her buckle shoes, dress and white cap. So, a towel wouldn't change anything. "Relax, Anita. We're on our Rumspringa remember? We are allowed to try these things," Noah said.

She nodded. Jedidiah went ahead to search the artist. A picture of a beautiful woman came up. Her hair was red with wide curls spanning over her head. She wore a sleeveless satin dress with the neckline revealing a bit of her cleavage and she leaned forward on a sofa chair in the picture. Anita knew she could never wear clothes like these, but she admitted the woman was beautiful. She suddenly began to imagine herself in such clothes. Stop it, Anita, she thought. A video of the Spice Girls began to play on the computer. It was slow and sweet. The women's voices reached into Anita's soul, causing her heart to trip in her ribcage. She's never heard such a beautiful angelic voice before. Yes, she had the voice of an angel. God blessed people with different gifts. Lizzy and Anita where both upset that they where not able to listen to them at home.

When the song ended, she wished it would be played over and over again. She wanted to snatch the mouse from Jedidiah and replay it. But they would use it to taunt her for ages. So, she replayed the tune she'd stored in her memory over and over again. Noah took over this time. Immediately his fingers touched the keys of the keyboard, he typed: PLUTO. The screen loaded for a while before its information popped up. Anita watched Noah's eyes quickly lap up all the information on the screen. Slowly, the blood drained from his face, turning him pale. "What's... wrong?" Lizzy said. Anita watched his mouth drop open and his eyes glossed over with unshed tear. She adjusted on her seat and looked at the others as if to confirm she was also seeing the same thing as they were. Confusion settled in her chest. "Pluto... is no longer a planet?" he whispered and then looked at them. Anita didn't know what to say. Or if she was even supposed to say anything. She remembered from the short time she was in school about the planets surrounding the sun. Pluto was among them. Noah talked about Pluto sometimes and how he would fly there if he could. But she didn't know it was this serious. Jedidiah leaned over and read the information on the screen. "The American government and NASA had declared that Pluto is not fit to be a planet," he read.

"So, they think they can deceive people any time they like," Noah said.

"Why is Pluto not fit to be a planet?" Lizzy said.

"Something about being too small," Jedidiah said.

"The American government is to blame for this. It is either they were lying before or they are only trying to deceive us," he said in a whisper.

They all drew closer to listen to him. "I know, I've read it. The government hides a lot of things from the public. They might be hiding something on Pluto, "Nobody said anything in reply. It was Noah after all. He could be wrong, right or crazy. It was when they'd gone back to the apartment and he suddenly called a meeting, making an absurd announcement that they thought he was mad. He clasped his palms under his chin and said, "I am making a robot."

Chapter Five

Noah was pissed. No, pissed was an understatement. He was boiling. Since they'd returned from their so called scouting, he had packed the room multiple times that evening. Jedidiah was starting to look worried. If he continued like this, his legs would give out under him. Noah's brain was working at full speed. He had never been embarrassed like that in his life. And what was worse? They were embarrassed for being Amish. There was simply no suitable reason why they had been rejected from being served food and a customer disgraced them in front of everybody. No matter how much he thought about it, there was no reason at all.

Then there was the news about Pluto not being a planet. Noah prided himself as a factual and logical person. He could even call himself a scientist. No one came close in their community. All his life, somewhere in his head, it had been stuck like paper. Pluto was a planet. His favorite planet for a specific reason. It had been his dream to study it and find out more about it someday. For a small planet, it was usually forgotten. Never given the time if the day. Now, they were saying it suddenly isn't a planet? He let out a noise from his throat. The American government. NASA

They were the ones that'd stripped Pluto of its title. Something was up. From the many conspiracy theories he'd heard about America and its government, he was a hundred percent sure they hid a lot of things from the public. What if there was gold on Pluto? What if the government was going to send a secret spaceship to extract the gold and become stupidly rich? As the thought settled into his brain, his stomach soured. Americans... So far they'd managed to ruin his day in the space of five hours. They were just like the government. Selfish and lacking warmth. They did what they wanted to do; they acted like they owned the world and behaved like anyone who wasn't like them was an oddity. He saw the way they littered their environment without care. He saw the way they spoke over each other, throwing curses at each other. He saw the way they prided luxury above any other thing. There was a divide. Beggars and homeless people slept near expensive restaurants and hotels.

It would never happen in the Amish society. Regardless of all their lack of technology, they still shower up for each other. His food was everybody's food. His house was their house. Nothing was hidden. They shared their problems and solved them together. Nobody was left stranded. He had to admit, even with all the fascinating technology, it was a cold world out her. The thought of the scene at the restaurant came to his mind again. He wasn't going to let it slide that easily. The people in the restaurant had trampled on them like they were ants. He was going to teach them a lesson. All of them. Both the government and the Americans.

He took a deep breath and sat on the bed, staring at a spot on the wall. Jedidiah, who was on the top bunk, popped his head over the bed to look at Noah. "Noah…" he called. Noah kept mute. He was in the zone. In his own world. Theories and thoughts zipped about in his mind. He zoned his concentration to the spot on the wall, looking for that solution. That spark that would come alive in his mind. And then, "Eureka!" he suddenly said, snapping his fingers. He bounced on his feet, light flooding his features as if a bulb sat on top of his head. Immediately, he went to the other room, called the girls' in for a meeting and when he was settled, he declared, "I am making a robot." There was pin-drop silence in the room for some seconds. Anita broke it. "Why are you making a robot and what is it supposed to be for? In fact, what is this all about?"

"You know how I said I didn't know what I wanted to do yet? I have found it. We're going to take our revenge with the robot I will build," Noah said. Jedidiah jumped down from the bunk. He had a curious spark in his eyes like Noah as expected. Deep down, Noah thanked God Jedidiah was his friend. If he was only left with Anita, he wouldn't have a lot of motivation to go through with his inventions. "How are you planning on doing that? Tell us more?" Jedidiah said. "Okay," Noah adjusted in his seat, drawing closer. On impulse, the rest drew closer. "Here's the plan. I will build a robot that looks like a human and I'll name it KAREN. When I'm done with it, I will release it into the world. Well, I'll release it to the restaurant for starters. It's going to cause havoc at the place and boom! Revenge." He splayed his fingers. "I don't know…" Anita said, "It sounds so absurd."

"Yeah, I think the same," Lizzy said. "How are you going to create a human-looking robot?" "Have faith in me," Noah said. Honestly, he was shocked the amount of faith he had in himself. Back at the abandoned shed, he'd been tinkering as usual and he was able to create a robot. It was as small as a phone's box and still unfinished, peeking with wires and scrap metals. He controlled it with a remote as he studied from the book and he was able to make it. "Listen," he continued. "I've tried to make a robot before at the shed and I did fairly well. We are now exposed to the internet and tons of knowledge around us. We can use it to our advantage. Think about it. It would be massive project for us. We just need metals, motors, tools, electrical things and all. We can get those. In fact…" he grinned, "I brought a lot of those things here too. We can get some more." All through, Jedidiah was nodding his head like an excited puppy. "So that's what you've been hiding in that bag of yours," he said.

Noah chuckled. "Well, they're precious to me." So, Jedidiah was definitely on his side now. He needed all the help he could get now. Lizzy was an easy person to convince. His main challenge now was convincing Anita to join them. If the three of them were in agreement, Lizzy would automatically join in. Noah sighed. "Think about what they did to you today. Was it fair on you? It's just treating them the same way they treated you. They stepped all over you for defending the Amish community." His speech was working. He could see it in the way her eyes suddenly lit up with a fire. He continued. "We should give them a taste of their own medicine and we should do it in style. What do you think?" He turned to Jedidiah. "Yeah, I'm in." Jedidiah hi-fived Noah.

"I'm in too," Lizzy said, "I did feet so helpless at the restaurant. I wanted to do something." All eyes turned to Anita. Her face was stony. His heart began to sink. Then she smiled. "You bet I'm in!" The room erupted in joyous shouts. They hugged each other and bounced around, letting the joy fill their hearts. After that, Noah pulled out a sheet of paper. "Now, to the plan." He spread it on the floor and they all sat around it. He began to draw up tasks and designs for them to follow. He gave each of them a task. Collecting scraps, scouting for an electronics shop, looking for an abandoned head model in the trash and getting information from the internet. He assigned tasks and they set to work for the week. For the important parts, he would need for the robot; he used his money to purchase them. Motors, transmitters and so on. They spent the whole week attending to their tasks and delivering as much as possible. The people at the dump gave them weird looks whenever they arrived, but with time, the Englishers got used to them.

In the second week, the production began, they all huddled together ad Noah mapped out the process step by step. Sometimes he had to stop and marvel at his own work. Marvel at his mind and audacity. No one he knew was able to beat their chest and declare that they were making a robot. But he was doing it. When he needed assurance, he would go to the internet café and watch videos of experts making robots and see how they did it. Then he would go home, rework and re-plan the process into his design and keep improving it. Slowly, the robot began to come into shape. The fruit of their hard work was becoming evident day by day. Most of his money, he'd spent on the tools and important parts. The rest of the money was used to get their groceries and other utilities they needed. It was finally time for him to test the robot with electricity. He had earlier constructed a connection of wires inside the metal trunk of the robot. It was just him and Jedidiah in the room now. He took two wires, peeled the rubber covering off with a plier exposing the metal twine inside. Then, he connected them through the openings in the switch.

"Fingers crossed. Let's pray this works," Noah said and Jedidiah nodded. Noah flicked the switch on. Instantly, there was a spark. And then, boom!! Noah and Jedidiah flew backwards, shielding themselves from the impact. The smell if smoke and melted plastic stung their nose. But that wasn't the main problem. Their light had gone off. Noah scurried to his feet and ran to the balcony, checking for the bulb in the balcony beside. The light was off. He check all the ones around him, they were off. "Jedidiah…" he said, eyes mirroring the fear in his eyes. "We're done for." There was a total black out in the apartment. Noah began to think fast as usual. "They're going to trace the explosion from here," Noah said. He started out of his frozen state and began to pack the tools.

Jedidiah joined him immediately. "Come on, quickly," Noah said. There was a knock on their door. His heart leapt into his throat. They paused and looked at each other, their eyes communicating what they both feared.

"Noah, Jedidiah! What's going on in there?" It was Anita's voice. They heaved a sigh of relief and Noah sprung towards the door and wrenched it open. He grabbed Anita's shoulders, startling her. "Quick! Help us. We have too hide the robots in your room before someone else comes here." Anita tucked away all her question and set to work. He respected her so much for that. Soon, they were carrying the bulky robot in all it is unfinished electrical and metal glory. They crossed the distance between the two room's quick and entered Anita's room with a crash. Lizzy who was sleeping, woke up with a crash. "What's going on?" she said. "No time to explain. We'll tell you later." Jedidiah said

"The explanation better make sense," ANITA said. They left her behind. Back in their room, they made sure to tidy the place. Then they waited and waited. Finally, there was a knock. Their prepared poses shattered immediately. Noah swallowed the lump in his throat and opened the door. Jedidiah's aunt stood there, a flat expression on her face. Her piercing eyes sent chills down her spine. "Something happened here?" she said, wandering the length of the room. "Yes, the switch suddenly sparked" He didn't finish the sentence; she suddenly drew close to him, placing her face inches away from his, closing the gap between them considerably. He could see the dull white of her eyes. She drew her head closer, eyes wide as if she was looking for something. He drew back. "Suddenly?" she said. "Yes, suddenly," Noah replied, his voice a whisper. "Hmm," she mused and looked around again. Then pinned her gaze on Jedidiah. "I'm watching you," she said. She backed away, towards the door and as soon as she closed the door behind her, they heaved a breath of relief. "That was close," Noah said, feeling half-guilty for lying.

Chapter Six

Anita and Lizzy were sitting in their room as Noah narrated everything to them. She'd heard the explosion from her room and left everything she was doing to rush to theirs. Of all the things in the world, she didn't think it would be because of the robot. They were so close to getting caught. What if Jedidiah's aunt had decided to come up earlier? She clutched her chest and groaned, relieved. It would have been a total disaster. They would be on their knees by now, begging for mercy. They would be thinking of how to pool money to fix the electricity problem. Along with being viewed as odd, people would see them as nuisances too. She shuddered at the thought. "Thank God, you were not caught," she said.

Noah nodded. "Right now, there is no electricity. So, I can't continue with the robot just yet. The next stage is paused for now," he said. So, he was still thinking about the robot. She shook her head. Anita just hoped this kind of adventure they'd chosen was not going to be a big problem in the future. She was well aware of how big and complex the modern world worked. They had laws she had to follow and enforcement agencies to keep them in check. She hoped they were not going against some law out there. And she hoped the landlady would never find out the truth behind the explosion. "I have a question," Lizzy said. We turned out attention to her. "What if you had actually get caught making the robot? What do you think would've happened? How would you have handled it?" There was silence for a while with each of them in their own worlds.

Anita played with the possibility in her head for some seconds. A lot of horrible things popped up. She couldn't even think of a solution to that. They were done for. From nowhere Jedidiah spoke up. "We can blackmail her." His words hung in the air like a suffocating perfume. "Meaning?" Noah said. "I mean, she deals with drugs. Hard drugs like cocaine," Jedidiah said. That explains things. He continued, "It's a family secret. If she exposes us, and the government or the police find out we're making a robot in our room, they might get us jailed. So she has to keep our secret in exchange for keeping hers too." A chill ran down her spine. It was this serious? She stood on her feet. "Everybody, this has become too risky. We can't continue with this."

Noah crossed his arms. "We've come this far to just stop. We made a mistake, I admit it. But we've learnt from it. We only have to be more careful next time." Anita was about to speak when Lizzy butt in. She stood up and raised her arms. "Wait. Before you two start your bickering. Since there is going to be lack of electricity now, I say it's a blessing in disguise. We have time to think about what we're doing and come to the conclusion. This period, our focus will be on other things until the building is fixed." We looked at each other. There was no sign of objection. I sighed and nodded. The Amish community probably saw something when they banned electricity. She was seeing it now. The room was calmer now, the tension had lessened. "There's an issue though," Anita said. "What is it this time?" Noah said. She rolled her eyes and continued. "We are running short on money. After this last batch of grocery shopping, we're going to be completely penniless." Jedidiah released an audible sigh and leaned back on the bunk. "So, what do you suggest we do?"

"We're going to have to find a job, of course. It's part of the Rumspringa experience, don't you think?" Anita replied. "I agree, there's no way to even contact our parents for money. We'd have to travel all the way back home," Lizzy said. Without further ado, they all agreed they should go out to look for jobs. The next day, they were all ready and in their usual Amish dressing. The stares were getting pretty annoying. To her surprise, Anita suggested they get normal clothing from the cloth stores instead of wearing their uniform and sticking out like a sore thumb. Surprisingly as well, they took the suggestion in good faith.

They didn't have money yet but when they have money, they would try on new clothes. Another experience to look forward to. All the weeks they'd spent touring the place for scraps and other things were not in vain. They were now much more familiar with the area and where things were. They had seen another restaurant on another street during their scouting. So they were going there to apply for jobs. All four of them. They reached the place. Anita stopped them before they could enter. "Wait, let's pray." They gathered and she said a short prayer, asking for favor and good luck in their endeavors. After they said their amen, they entered the restaurant. A bell at the top of the door pinged, signifying their entry.

Instantly, all eyes were pinned on them. Anita tried to hide the annoyance on her face. It was just a different style of dressing. Why were they so surprised? And they openly stared too. No shame at all. Noah stepped forward and asked to meet the person in charge. The people manning the counter and those who were working in the kitchen kept glancing at them. In a few minutes, a bulky man came out of an office tucked away in a hidden corner. She didn't even know there was a room there. "Yes? I'm the manager. Who's looking for me?" the man said to no one in particular as his eyes roamed the restaurant and then landed on the four of them. He frowned. "Are you the ones looking for me?" Noah stepped forward. "Yes, Sir. Good afternoon."

The man eyed him in return. Noah cleared his throat and spoke with confidence Anita thought she would have never mustered in front of those eyes. "We're looking for a job and we want to know if you can accept us to work under you… Sir." He quickly added. The silence that followed was deafening. Suddenly, he barked into laughter. It went on for so long, even other people began to laugh. His rumble shook his stomach as he hunched over his sides and slapped the counter, tears springing in his eyes. Anita wished the ground would just open and swallow them up. She bit her lips and stared the ground boring holes in them. They'd been made objects of ridicule once again.

The man slowed to a stop, wheezing and coughing. He flicked the tear from his eyes, took one step forward and said, "No." She took in a sharp breath. Even if she was expecting it, it dealt her a blow in her chest. "What we're you expecting?" He said, eyeing us one by one. "I mean you look like you rear chickens for a living and live in a sixteenth century farm. Your delivery is total trash as well. You should be submitting a CV, calling me out to propose to me." At this the restaurant laughed. "Get your scum selves out of my restaurant," he said as a note of finality and walked back to the office. The waiters and cooks dispersed, the customers turned back to their foods and they were left to stand there like fools. "Let's go," Noah turned to face them. His voice grazed her ears like concrete

She instantly became afraid. This darkness swirling in his eyes. She'd never seen it before. She worried what he might've been thinking in that moment. "Oh, dear Lord, help us," she muttered a prayer to the skies. Usually as they scouted the area, they would pass an open park. Anita loved the smell of the fresh grass whenever they passed by. It was there that they decided they would rest. The four of them sat on the bench, thinking over the incident that'd happened earlier. Children rushed past blowing bubbles and filling the air with their laughter. Cars and bicycles sped past. It was as if the world didn't care there were four Amish people who were feeling so devastated. The thought angered Anita. Everywhere they turned, it was like the whole world was against them. She couldn't see the Amish people living with rude people like these. It infuriated her, how much they were able to get under her skin.

"Ugh! I am so annoyed!" Lizzy spoke. Jedidiah kicked a stone sitting innocently on the grass. Noah on the other hand, he just stared ahead. This was his brooding state. "What do we do now?" Lizzy said. Anita had thought ahead of them. With the kind of reception she'd gotten from the street and the restaurant, she knew it would be a slim chance for them to be given jobs. So, she'd thought of a plan B. "I have an idea," They slightly turned to face her. Noah still stared ahead. "Instead of going around looking for jobs, why don't we give ourselves a job. Our community teaches baking as an important part of our studies. We can bake things like doughnuts or buns and sell them," she said. She could see the light return to Lizzy's eyes. "Yes. I can bake as well."

"Where are we going to sell it?" Jedidiah asked.

"We can sell it downstairs. Outside the apartment. Erect a stall like we did during the holiday season. Of course, we'll ask your aunt for permission," Anita said, detailing her plan to them. She was not as smart and complicated as Noah in making plans, but she did have a few tricks up her sleeves as well. "I'm up for it," Lizzy said. Jedidiah hugged half-heartedly. Noah still remained mute. She patted his shoulder. "Cheer up," she said. He nodded and sighed. The sun was starting to say its last goodbyes for the day. They had sat on the benches watching the benches and throwing stones to see who could throw the farthest. Evening was already upon them and with that, they had to keep moving.

They'd seen daytime in the city, but they'd not really seen night time. Neon lights began to appear all over. Other normal lights shone from the windows of glass buildings. The cars increased on the streets, the light illuminating the place. Headlights glared on the streets. To fight off the darkness, the city put lights everywhere. They were passing a bar. She knew because the music from inside pounded against their ears and somehow the stench of a strongly fermented drink reached her ears. "Let's try alcohol," Noah said all of a sudden. Her eyes almost bulged out of their sockets. She looked to her friends to gauge their expressions, but, they had curiosity glinting in their eyes. "You know…" Lizzy mused, tapping her lips. "I've always wondered what it tasted like since they're so against it at the community."

"Me too," Jedidiah said. "Great. So we're all in?" Noah said and then looked at her. She sighed. These people were taking her past boundaries she wouldn't even think of passing. "Alright, alright." "We're not staying her though. Just buy a bottle and let's move. This place makes me feel uncomfortable," Lizzy said. "Sure. We're definitely not staying here. Not at all," Noah said.

Chapter Seven

Noah ambled towards the entrance of the bar with his friends following behind. He had never been inside a bar before, but he was able to add to and two together and walk over to the counter. The man in a uniformed cloth watched them as they assembled in front of him. As expected, the man looked at them with some kind of wonder and curiosity. Noah was starting to totally hate it. Enough of them looking at him like he was out of this world. He was just a normal human being with different clothes. The situation at the restaurant had set him off completely. The sheer audacity if these people to look down on them for no reason. He couldn't understand it. Was this the society people boasted about? They talked like the country was the best thing to come out of earth. Where was it? This best thing? Best thing his foot.

That man had ridiculed them in front of the customer tore them layer by layer and made them a laughing stock to the problem. For the first time in his life, he was the subject of mockery. He was surrounded by people laughing in his face, mocking him. Nothing could be more traumatizing than that. With everything that had happened, he was not prepared for that at all. The bar had a cool ambience about it. Soft jazz music played somewhere and the blue-colored lights swung everywhere, illuminating the room. The stool is wooden protected by a sheen layer that made it gleam in the night. Behind the counter, different glasses in different shapes were arranged in rows. "I want to buy alcohol," he declared.

Not once since he entered the bar did he look back. He needed to steel himself against his friends. If he saw a slight waver in their resolute expressions, he would also waver. So, he made sure his back was to them. He heard alcohol took a person's mind away from things. So, he was willing to try it out. If not for the experience, then for the fact that it made people forget. The bar man paused and then as if snapping out from a trance, he nodded. "Which one would you like?" Noah paused to think. The place really looked so lavish, meaning things could be expensive. Besides, he didn't have an iota of knowledge about alcohol. "Give me the cheapest one," he said.

The bar man disappeared and then appeared with a bottle in his hand. Noah paid for it and he wordlessly left the place, still not giving them a glance. It must've been an odd sight. Four people in an exquisite-looking bar. Two of them with puffy unflattering plain dresses, a white cap and buckled shoes. While the other two wore black felt hats, a shirt and suspender pants with buckled shoes as well. Noah almost laughed at the imagery. Finally, the moon was high in the sky when they reached the apartment. They gathered in Anita's room this time. They all sat on the floor. The bottle of alcohol set in the middle. The robot was in a corner and where Noah sat, he was looking straight at it. He shifted his gaze, willing himself not to look and remember the other day they almost got caught. As stupid as it was, looking at his unfinished robot project made him feel like he was a failure. It ate at his chest, making him feel inadequate. Lizzy had brought the cups. "I wonder how this would tastes," Jedidiah said.

"Are we really going to do this?" Anita said. "Yes," Noah declared. He opened the bottle and poured small quantities inside the cup first just for them to see how it tasted. "Okay, on the count of three. We're going to drink it," he said. He looked at their expectant expressions, locking eyes and transferring his determination to them. "One... two... three!" In unison, they down the liquid. It burned through his throat leaving a fermented taste on his tongue and it settled in his stomach in an odd way. It was bitter too. He squeezed his face. Other made disgusted sounds or strangling sounds from the taste and feel of it. Even with all these, there was something strangely addictive about the taste. He poured another one in his cup. This time, he filled it halfway. "You like it?" Anita said, giving him an incredulous look. He shrugged. "I'm not sure, but I would like to taste it again."

They watched him as he gulped the drink down again. He made a satisfied "ah" sound and slammed the cup on the floor. Again, he reached out and poured another one much to their surprise. He filled his cup to the brim and then drank it to the last drop. Something was happening to him. First his limbs felt heavier, like her was wading through a mighty ocean and it was dragging him back. His vision became to blur and his mind began to work slowly. He felt like he was floating. Floating away. Above everything. "What's wrong with me?" he slurred. "What do you think?" Jedidiah said, "You drank like half a bottle of alcohol." He was crossing his arms. The voice sounded like Jedidiah to Noah, but it didn't quite sound like Jedidiah to him. So, he looked up to confirm who was talking. Then his eyes met the robot.

Memories and events came crashing back in his mind. He remembered why he had decided to create the robot in the first place. The humiliation he faced from the hand of the Americans, their general behavior, the fact that the government was covering up something on Pluto. It all came crashing back. He was not a loose-mouthed person. He usually kept his thoughts to himself, but suddenly, he found himself speaking those thoughts he kept to himself. "The American government is lying about Pluto. Pluto is still a PLANET!" He yelled. The shocked expressions of his friends swam in front of him. He chuckled. "Why do you look so scared?" he said. Then looked at the robot. "I'm going to finish you, robot. And when I do, I will get my revenge. Is rest assured about that. Stupid piece of metal." He threw his cup towards the robot. It slammed the body and clattered to the floor.

"Hey, hey, Noah." Somebody held his hands. He looked up to meet Jedidiah's eyes "Jed?" "Hmm?" "We're going to build a robot right? "Yes, Noah. Yes we will," Jedidiah replied. His reassurance assured Noah, filling his heart with peace and satisfaction. He slumped in Jedidiah's arms and blacked out. With Anita's new plan about baking pastries and selling it, life came back to their rooms. Noah didn't go an hour without wallowing in the scent of vanilla coated doughnuts and buns. If the smell could make him salivate so much, then it was positive that they were in the right direction. Like magic, they attracted customers from all over the place. The stand had been built with a table and two poles by the side holding up a banner. While Lizzy and Anita were in their rooms whipping up the delicacy, Jedidiah manned the stand and sold the pastries.

Sometimes, Noah did, but he was not busy with the robot as they'd finally fixed the electricity problem. Now more than ever, he was as careful as anything. He made sure to check the proper calculations and measurements, ensuring accuracy to the best of his abilities. From the profit they made from sales, they bought more ingredients to bake more pastries, they paid Jedidiah's aunt her fee and Noah was able to buy some of the materials he needed. The robot was slowly coming to completion. He had melted plastic and molded it into a human face then he covered it with material that looked like and had the same properties of human skin. It wasn't perfect, but it was enough. Finally, after many weeks and frustrations and despair, the robot was ready. It was covered with a blue gown from head to the very toe where it was just a treadmill type of machine for movement.

He covered the robot's mouth with a mask and then added sunglasses. Then, he sewed in blonde weaves to the head to give it the perfect overall Karen look. "Wow!" Lizzy exclaimed when she saw the finished work. "Oh my, this is amazing. We've got a genius on our hands guys." Noah smiled. He'd done all the test runs he needed to do. Now it was time to put their plan in motion. He called all of them together. "Guys, we are going to take our revenge. Who is excited!!" They whooped and cheered. This was a defining moment for them. Their Rumspringa was giving them the opportunity to create this moment and they were not going to waste any of it. They would execute their plan at the break of dawn. They picked the date and anticipated. Once it came, they were ready. The four of them emerged from the apartment with the masked robot. The robot glided beside them as Noah controlled it with a remote. They wanted to look as natural as possible, so they put Noah at the other end of the line away from the robot as he controlled the remote.

People gave them weird looks. The bunch was strange, but they didn't seem to know what exactly it was. They would stop, stare at them for some seconds, shrug and then carry on. Soon, they reached the restaurant. Seeing the building brought memories to Noah's forefront. He was determined now. The embarrassment they'd faced fueled his bones with anger. They hid in an alley that gave them a perfect view of the restaurant. Noah had installed a speaker that was programmed in a lady's voice around the mouth area that was covered with the mask. So, Noah would be the one to speak. He controlled the remote carefully guiding the robot past the intersection and into the restaurant. With the camera inserted in the robot's eye, Noah could see the view in her periphery. "Hi, how can I help you?" A waiter walked up to her with a smile. But as she neared, the smile faded, replaced with confusion that she tried to mask but failed.

"Can you let me sit first?" Noah said into the microphone. "Oh are you going to force me to buy food?" The waiter looked dumfounded. She tried to find words but failed to articulate herself well. "Why are you just standing there?" Noah said. The other customers were now looking at the scene in front of them "I'm sorry, I leave you. There's a menu on the table," she said. "I know there's a menu on the table, I had an education unlike you." Anita gasped beside him just as the waiter gasped and slapped a palm across her face. The others looked at him in shock. Oh, they'd not seen anything yet. He was just getting started. He had spent weeks planning this, this was his time to shine. He had created something out of nothing. He had invested so much into it. He even got drunk because of them. He wasn't going easy. Overcoming his shock, Jedidiah cheered him on. He was clearly enjoying it as much as Noah did. They served the robot a coffee as per his request. He had prepared a small something to add to the coffee. He ejected a fake spider into the coffee.

Then, he began to scream into the mic, passersby must've heard them, but the alley way wasn't somewhere most people would like to explore. Waiters rushed to the robot's side. It was stiff as usual making no movement, but it spoke as he'd planned. "There is a spider in my drink," the robot yelled. The color vanished from their faces. The customers had become uncomfortable on hearing the news.

Chapter Eight

Anita watched the scene unfold in front of them. She admitted she felt a thrill of excitement. For once, she wasn't following the rules. They were doing whatever they wanted and it was a wonderful feeling. Like being set free from a cage. She could feel her wings grow and if she just spread them apart, she would soar. There was no looking behind her shoulders, there was no trying to keep to time. It was just her and her friends having fun. She looked at their face, the pure joy beaming from their smiles was unmatched. She never had seen them ooze such freedom. She smiled to herself and huddled even closer to watch the screen Noah held.

The waiters hurried about in a shaken frenzy as they took the spider-infested drink and sang apologies to the robot. She immediately saw the waiter who had refused them entry and a rush of adrenaline spiked through her veins. She grabbed the remote control out of Noah's hands. "Let me speak this time," she said. Noah studied her for some seconds and slowly, a smile grew on his lips. He nodded and gave her leeway. The rest surrounded her. "Ma'am we're so sorry about that. This has never happened before at the restaurant. We're very particular about hygiene and sanitary precautions," the waiter said. Anita's frown deepened. The waiter was acting like a saint here, treating the robot like a customer should be treated and spoken to. The fear in her eyes was palpable and she wrung the towel hanging from her waist every now and then.

"How do I know you're not lying? That is a rehearsed speech, isn't it? I should write a review on this restaurant," Anita said into the mic. She'd read so many reviews of restaurants in the newspapers so, she knew a bad review would rile them up. "No, no, no, ma'am. You don't have to do this," the waiter waved her hands in the robot's face frantically. "I assure you we are one of the best in this neighborhood. I think the spider did not come from our kitchen. Maybe it fell from somewhere." "So, are you saying I put it there?" The robot said as Anita increased the tone of her voice. "No, that's not"

Anita controlled the robot so it stood. "Where is your manager. I will like to see him or her." Anita said into the mic again. All her life, Anita had prided herself as a fairly good person. She refrained from treating people bad and followed the Bible's teachings on turning the other cheek. But, when she saw the color leave that waiter's face, satisfaction settled in her heart pleasantly. Pushing the guilt that was starting to creep up away, she gripped the remote harder and an evil smile found its way to her lips. "Um…" the waiter looked around at the expectant eyes of the customers and the dread in the eyes of the other workers. "He is not on seat at the moment." "Ha!" Anita let out a mocking laugh. "Poor food hygiene, poor service from the employees and an absent manager? Nothing could be worse than this? What a mess!"

"Wow, she's really in character," Jedidiah said beside her. Lizzy chuckled and Noah smiled. She controlled the neck so it could turn and face the customers. It was an unnatural twist of the neck, but there was something bigger compared to that that was grabbing attention and that was the scene in front of them. "Is this the kind of restaurant you people enjoy? This place is utter nonsense. It's not worthy to be called a restaurant and you—" she controlled the neck to face the waiter, "—are not worthy to be called a waiter or a job owner." Lizzy gasped beside her, slapping her palm over her mouth. "Woah!" the two guys chorused their shock. Anita grinned. "An eye for an eye." She moved the knobs on the controller, moving the robot to the counter, where the spider-infested drink had been place. The waiter followed after her. "Ma'am wait"

In a split second, the robot's hand shot out and knocked the glass off the counter, spilling the drink on her uniform. At this point, tears formed a sheen over the waiter's eyes. Her mouth dropped open as she stared at the stain on her shirt. People had risen on their feet, also wearing shocked expressions. The waited snapped out of her shock and with a sob, ran off to the back inside the kitchen. Anita had attracted a lot of attention now. The waiters had been trying to please the robot, but she could now see their scalding looks directed at her. Before one of them could walk up to her and ask her to leave, she said into the mic, "Good riddance." Then, she made an unnatural turn with the robot and led it outside the restaurant, across the street and towards the alley where they hid. "What?" she finally said when she became aware of the silence from the other three. "That was… wow," Noah said. "I've never seen this side of you before," Jedidiah said. "Now, I'm scared of you," Lizzy chuckled nervously and scratched the back of her neck.

"Come on, guys. It's still me," Anita laughed, though she couldn't help the uneasy feeling rising up in her heart. She had said a lot of things and acted unlike herself. Perhaps she had even gone too far, spilling the drink on the waiter. In that moment, she was like a completely different person. She'd let another side take control of her. She bit her lips and handed the remote back to Noah. Maybe restrictions were alright once in a while. She'd always ran after Noah, trying to keep him in check so he won't explode and jump into some kind of trouble. But nobody was there to restrict her. Not like there was anything to be restricted. Or so she thought. The realization dawned on her. The Or dung, Amish laws guiding the community were always restricting her. This was what kept her in check and she submitted to it wholly.

Not wanting to spoil the mood with her thoughts and expressions again, she put up a smile and said, "I guess we all have that part of us in there somehow." Soon they got over their shock. Noah was not done with the robot yet. He had other plans. They were going to take it for a stroll according to him. What he said next though, made her uneasy. Something about terrorizing the bad Americans. Like loyal sheep, Lizzy and Jedidiah agreed to it. So the journey began. If Noah saw someone litter the ground, he would make the robot follow them, yelling over their heads how they were so dirty and worse than pigs. Most of the people ran off, terrified by the menacing person following them. Some looked over their backs with disdain and others just stared as Noah continued on his tirade. Their robot was getting popular on the street. The neighborhood Karen who wore a mask and sunglasses, putting everybody I checked. Most of the time the group bright ideas normally came to them while they where on the People Mover. They would eat chili cheese fires and ride around pointlessly because it helps them come up with ideas. Also they became addicted to chili cheese fries and like going fast.

They had their fill of their fun for days until one day when they came across a bunch of high school bullies harassing a classmate. The sight deeply annoyed Anita. And from the look on her friend's faces, they also hated what they were seeing. Thankfully, the apartment wasn't too far. They were on a stroll without the robot, so they turned back to get it. Hiding behind a park bench, they led the robot to the crime scene. "Hey, what do you guys think you are doing?" Noah spoke into the mic, drawing their attention to the robot. The one with the bulkiest frame who seemed like the leader, stepped forward, a sick grin in place. Anita thought the way his hair fell over his eyes was stupid. Recently, she'd thought a lot of the American fashion sense was simply stupid. They wore a lot of unnecessary and uncomfortable things all in the name of looking fashionable. The boy's hair falling over his face was obviously going to impair his vision somehow. And it was evident in the way he pushed his hair back occasionally.

"Well, well, well. If it isn't the popular Karen. What you gon' do now? Beat us up?" He said, looking behind at his minions. There was a pause and suddenly, they all burst into laughter that sounded fake to her ears. Pathetic. "Leave the boy alone and I won't touch you," Noah threatened. This seemed to work with most people. The robot could barely do much in terms of mobility, but the rumors going about in the neighborhood had made it out to be like Karen was a force to be reckoned with. So, people cowered and surrendered often. But it didn't work here. The guy stepped forward, his wide frame overshadowing the robot. "Or what?" Anita and her friend exchanged looks. This was new. They'd not planned for confrontation at all. It was silent where they were as they thought of what to do next. The boy looked like he was itching for something physical. If he made a made and swiped the mask and glasses off, it was over for them. They had to keep this secret under lock and key.

"What? Cat got your tongue? You can't speak now? Or you're just a chicken," he barked a laugh and then threw his head over his shoulders to look at his minion. There was a short pause and then they burst into fits of fake laughter. Anita gritted her teeth. The boy needed to be put in his place. He acted like he was king of the whole place. "Well, this is getting boring," he declared and then looked behind him. "Hey, TinTin, lemme have your juice." He popped his hand out. A boy slipped the juice into his hands. What is he…? Anita had no time to finish her thought. In a split second, right in front of their eyes, the boy poured the juice on Karen. Her mouth dropped open and her eyes threatened to bulge out of their sockets. Noah froze beside her as the remote slipped from his palms and clattered to the ground. Lizzy and Jedidiah let strangled sounds escape from their throats.

They watched in utter shock at the scene in front of them. The liquid seed through the breaks and crevices of the robot's neck, finding its way through the complexities of the metals, wires and motors. "What? No reaction too? Are you a robot?" the boy said. This time, there was no need to scare the minions. They laughed without any prompting. Anita's eyes never left the robot. Suddenly, there was a spark from the neck. The boys jumped back. Anita's heart dropped. Then a burning smell began to seep through from the hair on the robot's head. It was sharp, stinging her nose as tears sprung to her eyes. "Guys…" the boy took a step back. She could see the fear in his eyes. Worse than that of his minions. So much for being a leader. "I think we should run," he said.

As the statement left his lips, a loud bang rocked the park on its foundation. The robot exploded, its parts flying over the place, sending bits of metal, wire and plastic skin al over the place.

The boys shrieked and ran off in the other direction. While Anita and friends, huddled together, lowered themselves on the ground and covered their heads with their palms. A thud in front of them startled them. They raised their head in unison. Standing in front of them on the grass was the robot's head, hairless. Smoke still oozed out from the neck part and the face was half plastic and half metal. They all turned to look at Noah.

They were all afraid of saying something that would put something off. Anita threw glances at Noah. He wordlessly picked the scraps he could find. They did the same, combing the park quickly. This was after they had stayed there for thirty minutes, looking to see if anybody would show up to inspect the place. The boys might've run off and informed somebody about what they'd seen. Or people were just too scared of what they might find if they searched. After what seemed like an hour, they all trudged back to the apartment, their arms full of scraps. They gathered in Noah's room and they all sat thinking of what to say. Anita couldn't imagine how devastated Noah must've been. For weeks, he had sacrificed so much into building that robot. They'd fought over it, they'd risked being caught over it, they had gone broke over it and they were forced to be entrepreneurs because of it.

Only to see all their hard work goes down the drain in one second. Life wasn't fair. This was what Anita thought as she wiped her eyes with the back of her palms. It was so hard to build but easy to destroy. Why was it like that? Why did God make it to be so? Where would they start from now? Using the robot to bring some kind of order to the neighborhood had given their Rumspringa purpose. but as they sat there, she couldn't help but think it was all a waste. It would be better to just pack all their luggage and start going home to there normal life. So far, nobody has hinted at staying in this modern world. To her, it wasn't worth it. Their ways of life were different, but she was happier there compared to this world. Suddenly, Noah sighed and set his arms behind his head. All eyes turned to him. It was the only reaction they'd gotten since the incident.

"What do you think of the Americans?" he asked with a strange look in his eyes. Jedidiah took this question like a grain of salt. He shrugged. "I think they need to focus on more important things like bonding with your community and having a family. They're too obsessed with flashiness, "I agree," Lizzy said, "It is too much for me. It seems there is a hierarchy of some sort. People with more wealth are respected more and have power over those who are less than them in wealth. It sickens me."

Thinking about the bully, Anita had to agree. She spoke. "Yes, you're right. There is a lot of work to do in the American society. I will admit that there are a lot of things I would be interested in but this life is too fast-paced for me. I might not be able to catch up." Noah nodded. "For me, ever since I came here, I have been embarrassed, disappointed and disgraced by the Americans and their government. Everything about them has put me in a sour mood. Who knows if they're watching us right now. That is how the government is. They do not care for your privacy. If you pose even a small threat to them, you will be marked. Many people have even been assassinated because of this: telling the truth about them,"

Anita frowned in confusion. She didn't understand where he was heading to and why he was suddenly talking about this. As usual, Jedidiah was lapping up everything he said, nodding in agreement. She didn't understand those two boys. They were always in sync as if they shared the same brain. She sighed. "Get to the point, Noah." "Those guys destroyed my robot easily. They cannot get away with it easily. They have to pay for what they did. America has to pay for what it did. It is a blessing in disguise because I was able to see that our robot is not strong enough. We need something reliable. We cannot get it with just one robot.

Anita's heart tripped. She didn't want to jump to conclusion. She said the next thing on her mind, her voice betraying her fears. "So, what are you getting at?"

"We need to create robots on a large scale. We can have a large research center where we create thousands of Karen's. We need it to work. This is going to be our revenge. For Pluto and for us." Noah w.as un one of his new moods since the being of this vacation. Anita thinks he has been listening to too much music. She was blaming ODB who ever he was. For the reason that he keep whispering Wu-Tang is for the children. An keep putting up a W sign with his hands. Anita was on her feet immediately. She looked at Noah like he had grown two heads. "No. What are you even talking about, Noah." Mad. Noah was definitely mad. She didn't care that there were others in the room with them. Her brother needed to be engaged in an eye-opening conversation.

"What?" he said. "For Christ's sake, snap out of this. Wake up to your reality. Do you think it is easy to get a research center? And all those robots for what? What do you take us for. We're Amish for crying out loud. What are you doing?" she said and cast a heated gaze at her other two friends. She felt betrayed they were not siding her. Noah stood on his feet, mirroring her glare. "What is the

Rumspringa for? I'm asking you Anita. Why do you think we are here in the first place? Is it to sell pastries or cramp ourselves up in a room until we're tired of it? What? They let us loose, meaning we can dream big. We are not confined to the community anymore. It's not my fault you're a small-minded person." "Noah…" Lizzy whispered beside them. "Small-minded?" Anita replied. "No, I am a rational human being. You on the other hand, you are delusional. Have you forgotten that we almost got caught for just making one robot? Do you even understand the gravity of what you are saying? You are just a sixteen-year-old from an unknown Amish community? The world out here is so different and huge."

"And so, what? Am I not allowed to plan and dream? Didn't I think of making a robot? Did I or did I not work hard to make it a reality. Unlike you who depend on people to make things happen, I create things. Anita, you have grown up as a scared little girl and you have always followed me around trying to draw me back and quench my fire. But not today. Please, just leave me alone," he said and walked past her, out of the room. Tears burned at the back of her eyes and her chest twisted painfully. She grabbed fistfuls of her dress and marched out of the room as well. His words played in her mind. Small-minded? She barked a hollow laugh, ending in a sob. She needed to get out of the apartment and go somewhere else. Anita left the building completely and began to walk without any direction. She sniffed and tried to clear the knot in her throat. How could he be so rude to her? Everything she had done was in his best interest. She had to be the voice of reason in the group.

She cleared her throat and walked faster, past building, past statues, past parks and past cars. As the wind burned against her eyes, the tears began to drop, blurring her vision. She'd thought she was doing the right thing. She thought he appreciated her for looking out for him and keeping him off the deep end. But she was wrong. How long had he been holding on to the thought that she was a nuisance. She felt so stupid as the thought danced around in her mind. So, all the while, she had been making a fool of herself. He thought her to be a small-minded person, inferior to him. Yes, Anita knew he was a genius. He could invent things from scratch and make people marvel at his creations. But she'd never thought herself to be inferior to him. She was also a curious person who marveled at the complexities of the world and wished to know more. But, along with that curiosity, there was sensibility. She didn't let her desires cloud her sense of reasoning. That was what Noah was doing and that was what she was trying to save him from. She saw the internet café from afar. Confirming she had some money with her, she went there and found an empty spot. After settling into the chair and staring at the screen for too long, a fresh bout of tears poured from her eyes. She laid her head from the desk, sobbing silently.

Was she small-minded like he said? Anita tried to put herself in his shoes. Noah was a person who craved for knowledge like his daily bread. He surrounded himself with so many books, immersing himself in that world. When he left his books, he was drawn back to reality of who he was and where he was. He was torn between a great desire for something more and his reality. It must've have been frustrating. Wouldn't it have been better if he didn't discover his passion at all? So, he wouldn't have to fight himself. But life had other plans. He was deep into it before she could blink. He even had to make his inventing shed a secret from others. He had been hiding for a long time. The Rumspringa was his saving grace. The realization hit her like a bag of bricks. She whimpered and covered her mouth with her palm, stifling her sob. She, Anita, had been trying to snuff out his desire. She'd been trying to put him in a box. She had grown up in a box and she'd accepted it. But Noah had never accepted it and she was trying to force him to. Anita knew how much she hated being forced to do something. She sat up and wiped her tears. Noah talked about the power of the internet. It possessed a lot of answers to questions according to him. Remembering how Jedidiah had done it that day, she used the mouse to navigate the arrow until she found Google. They she typed into the search bar, "research center." A bunch of things popped up on the screen. The information was interesting, but it wasn't what she was looking for. She decided to be more specific.

"How to get a research center," she typed. She checked the answers that came up one by one until she came across something called a grant. These were funds that were given by charity organizations to people for a specific purpose. She was getting somewhere. Her heart raced. She quickly typed, "How to get a grant." She browsed the answers again. This time, her movements with the mouse were more fluid. She moved seamlessly, navigating the screen and its windows. She found out that people applied through letters. Grant application letters. Then, she saw a website with the list of available grants in that period. One of them caught her attention. Pell Grant. She opened the window. Applications were open now and it was going to be closing soon. She took the small note by the desk and wrote some instructions on the paper. She quickly stuffed the paper in her pocket and rushes back home. As she neared the apartment, she saw Noah coming towards the entrance from the opposite direction. They met in the middle, both of them avoiding their eyes.

"I'm sorry," they both said. Then they looked up at each other. "What are you sorry for?" Noah said in a small voice, throwing his gaze elsewhere. "I'm the one who was blabbing my mouth, saying stupid things. I didn't mean any of that." "No, I should've listened to what you wanted. I act like I'm mother a lot. I shouldn't try to stifle you," she replied. They didn't say anything after that. Somehow, they had come to a silent understanding without saying too much.

Chapter Nine

Noah had gone for the stroll with a lot on his mind and regret bubbling in his heart. He couldn't image he had said things like that to his sister. He let his anger take over and now he was paying dearly for it. Maybe the robot idea was a bad one. Come to think of it, they were all focused on his desire to make a robot. He didn't even care one bit about what they wanted and where they wanted to go. They were so invested in his design and he was too selfish to see it. He took a deep breath, tipping his hat over his head. He had to apologize, bother to Anita and his friends. Maybe have a new start and try something else. More than anything, he loved the bond he shared with his friends and it gave him life. He'd later come across Anita and they'd said their apologies.

A weight was lifted from his shoulders. Right now, he just wanted to clear the thought of the robot incident. He would try to listen more to his friends and not let his voice overshadow theirs. When he went upstairs, he asked everyone to gather in the room and faced them. "First of all, I want to apologize to Anita for what I'd said earlier. It was unlike me and I wish I could retract everything that I'd said. You're very valuable to the group and yes, we do need to be kept in check sometimes," he said. Anita smiled. "I hold no grudge against you. I was crass myself. I need to try and understand you better," she said. Jedidiah whooped and clapped his hands while Lizzy laughed. Noah could sense their connection coming back. The tension began to lessen with each second that passed and their laughter filled the air.

He missed this part of their hangouts. He clapped his hands twice, drawing their attention. "I also want to give a general apology. I've been so obsessed with the robot and I ignored you guys and what you wanted. I feel so selfish now, but I hope you can forgive me and we can move better in the future." "There is no grudge from me on this side. I enjoyed every step of the way and I really don't know what we would have done anyway," Jedidiah raised his palms and grinned. Lizzy nodded. "Well, about that," Anita drawled, reaching into her pocket. Noah's emotions heightened. They zipped under his skin, setting his heart off. Was she going to say she would not forgive him? She brought out a piece of paper and unfolded it. "I thought about the research center topic and went to the internet café to search more about it. I found this." She stretched out her arms with the paper lodged in between. He took it and read the details. "Pell grant?"

"Yeah, we can apply for it and get the research center as you said," Anita replied. Noah blanked for a moment. "Does this mean…" "Yeah.

It's out Rumspringa. When are we going to get the chance at a research center if not now?" she replied. "Let me see," Lizzy said and took it from his hands. Honestly, a part of Noah had shattered when he saw his robot blow up to pieces. He had tried to beef up his hope with the research center topic, but it looked too good to be true. And now, his sister was bringing a solution. He smiled at her, gratitude brimming in his chest. He wasn't going to forget this gesture ever. "It's a great idea!" Jedidiah said, giving Anita a thumbs up. Lizzy laughed. "I cannot actually believe we're trying to get funds for a research center."

"We can afford to have big dreams. It doesn't hurt anybody," Anita said with a smile. She was starting to be more accommodating and Noah loved this side of her. He knew he could be hard and complex sometimes, but she was trying to root for him and he cherished it. With a new focus in place, they decided Lizzy would write the letter. They would need someone who was good with words and Lizzy was just the person for that. Thankfully, while Anita was searching the web, she was taking note of what the essential parts of a grant were. And she gave that knowledge to Lizzy. For the next three days, they'd left Lizzy to herself as she worked on the grant application. They were going to go with half-truths and half-lies to help them. Of course, they weren't going to say they were creating robots to punish Americans, they were going to use the excuse of cleaning the environment and saving the earth from climate change or something like that.

Their sales of pastries were going well, although production was much slower with Lizzy writing and researching everything that was needed. At the third and final day, the letter was ready. Lizzy had them read through the letter and to Noah's surprise, it impressed him so much. It was like something he'd see in a Presidential file. Anita was excited the most talking about how Lizzy could write newspapers too. Noah knew the suggestion was out of this world. All people in their community stopped schooling in grade eight. This was the rule and they had to follow it. Without a university degree, there would be no writing in newspapers, but no one said a thing. Noah and Anita were going together to submit the application at a branch office. By now, they'd already gotten used to the curious stares and shielded looks thrown their way.

They managed to ask for directions to the place and thankfully they found the office. At first, the receptionist at the desk was skeptical about having their application. She eyed them suspiciously. Didn't even hide it. He didn't blame her at this point They were just two Amish teenagers applying for a grant offering thousands of dollars. But there was no criterion to submission, so she would have to accept theirs. They had been told they would get a reply in a month's time. The next month was something else entirely. They were all tensed, waiting for the news to arrive. Noah had hung up a calendar and he ticked it every day, reminding himself that the day was drawing near.

Their business was booming to their surprise. With the robot construction out of the way, all hands were on deck. There was no space for slacking. Another table had been added beside the first one to accommodate more pastries. If their parents saw them now, they would be so proud. More and more people began to get used to their presence. The curious gazes and malicious stares reduced considerably. They now looked forward to going on strolls. With the money they earned, they tried everything they could. From ice cream, to video game centers, to cinemas and parks, there was no space they didn't enter. Of course, it came with its own problems. Moving out of their neighborhood into newer spaces attracted massive attention. They stood out like a sore thumb. If they wanted an attention-free Rumspringa, they would really have to start considering getting new clothes now.

But since they went together, they were somewhat immune from the attention. There was something about being with your friends in a space. It gave confidence and put oneself at ease. Their adventures were enough to tear their minds away from the email reply, but unfortunately, like a thief in the night, a new month came. That morning they gathered round and held hands as Anita said a word of prayer. The result was going to make or mar their spirits. They reached the café and without wasting time, found an empty spot and put in the password their recently opened email. Apart from some spam emails, there was a prominent one.

PELL GRANT, it said.

Fingers crossed; Noah clicked the email open. He read it aloud,

Dear Noah and Anita Smucker,

We are sorry to inform you that your application to the Pell grant had been rejected. It was like a force slammed into his chest, stealing his breath from him. He gasped and continued scrolling with the mouse, this time with his hand shaking over it. The Pell grant is a fund, set up by the American government to invest in small scale business that can give profit and value. We do not find Amish people capable of giving us this value. This is in reference to your way of life and beliefs.

Once again, we are sorry and thank you for applying. The silence between them was heavy. Noah held his hands on his head, his breaths coming out shallow. They were rejected because they were Amish? Did he just read right? His fingers dug into his hat as he gritted his teeth. Instead of anger, he felt a resolve thicken within him. He would show them. Each and every one of them. He would make them pay for underestimating them.

The government would not hear the last of him. That he was sure of. While his friends muttered about how unlucky they were as they made their way home. He began to brainstorm, running through all the endless possibilities in his mind. He needed to come up with something. This wasn't the end of the road for them. Slowly, the workings of an idea began to grow in his mind. He would keep it to himself until they reached the apartment and he'd tell Jedidiah only. When he reached their room, he pulled Jedidiah to his side, "I have an idea," he said. "Wow. You never seem to stop coming up with those," Jedidiah said. But it wasn't with contempt, it was with excitement. Noah loved the reception he was getting. This is why he confided in Jedidiah. Anita would have drowned his morale. "Okay, this is it." He sat down along with Jedidiah. "I think we should recruit more hands."

"Really?" Jedidiah had an incredulous look on his face. He sighed and said, "I have supported you all the while but I don't think I understand you this time. Don't you think it is dangerous?" Noah shook his head before Jedidiah could finish. "We can try at least. There must be others out there like us." Jedidiah said, "So how are we going to go about it? What do you think we can do?" Noah came closer and whispered, "We are going to make flyers and paste them around the neighborhood. We are going to make coded flyers." "It's going to be in such a way that a person who sees it would be able to decode the message there and come to this apartment to meet us." Good old, Jedidiah, he agreed to it. In the next couple of days, they worked silently behind the girls' backs, creating flyers. Noah had come up with a message that had to be decoded before it was understood. He made sure to brainstorm really hard about this one because he didn't want just anybody to show up. In fact, he wasn't even sure somebody was going to show up but he had faith as usual. He always had faith. So, he did what he could.

The message to be decoded would only be gotten by those who were super smart, as smart as Noah and as calculated as Jedidiah. Those were the kind of people he was looking for. Those were the people who could understand him and be able to carry his dreams along with them. Not like Anita who hid from his dreams. He needed people who would face his ideas and run with him. On one fateful day that they had picked, they secretly left the apartment and began to paste the flyers on different buildings around the neighborhood. In Noah's heart he hoped that somebody would see it and they would decode it, finding their way to his room. He had said that prayer but he wasn't expecting that in the next couple of hours there would be a knock on their door and when he would open, a girl would be standing in front of him.

Chapter Ten

Noah stared at the girl. She blinked at him. They kept their gaze for more than ten seconds. Finally, he said, "Hello, do you have the wrong room?" She shook her head and tucked her hand inside the side pocket of her jeans, pulling out a flyer. When he saw it, his heart began to trip. He recognized it as his flyer. He looked at it and looked back at her. The confirmation in her eyes was all he needed to know. "You are here to join the group?"

"Yes," she said, "I have decoded it and I'm here because I am interested in whatever you guys are doing." Jedidiah called behind him, "Who is there?" Noah looked over his shoulders. He didn't know what to say. What was her name? As if she read his thoughts, he looked back at her and she said, "Rachel." She stood on her tippy toes and looked beyond Noah's shoulder. "Good day to you over there," she said. Jedidiah came closer. "Hello…" he looked at her and then back at Noah. Noah broke the silence, "She is here for the interview, Jedidiah." His mouth dropped open. It was evident even he wasn't expecting somebody to show up this fast. "So, can I come in?" she said. Noah nodded swiftly and moved aside letting her in. She stood at the center of the room inspecting the environment "Nice place," she said and nodded. "So, when am I going to start the interview?"

Noah stepped forward "I think right now. Yes, right now. Jedidiah are you going to interview her?" He asked him. Jedidiah shook his head and said, "It's okay, you can go ahead." Noah didn't understand why he felt so nervous. There was a sheen of sweat on his forehead. His words were stuck in his throat and his brain couldn't form coherent sentences. He drew the chair back away from the desk and offered to let her seat. When she sat, he in turn sat on the lower bunk bed, while Jedidiah leaned on the kitchen door watching the scene in front of him. Noah studied her and she also studied him openly. It was a battle of studying. Her hair was cropped by her neck and she had a black bang covering her forehead. Unlike most girls who preferred curly and wavy hair, hers was straight and short, a shiny black color. She wore round sleek black glasses as well and a black shirt on jeans trousers and black sneakers. He had never seen anyone who liked the black as much as this person. He was tempted to ask if she was married. In the Amish community, the married people always wore black. For some reason, he thought it would be a disappointment if she was indeed married.

His frowned and sat straighter. Why was he thinking like this all of a sudden? Taking more time to study her, he noticed that her eyes were had the same curiosity that he had found when he looked at

Jedidiah the first day, he met him. Her nose was straight like an eagle's talons and her lips were pressed together in a straight line. She placed her palms on her laps and waited for him to speak. He cleared his throat again. Something was definitely wrong with him. "Okay." He asked, "Why do you want to join us?" Without missing a beat, she replied, "Well, I think the code was impressive. It took a lot of time for me to decode it but I did in the end anyway. So, I wondered what kind of person would come up with something as complex as this and it sparked curiosity within Me. I decided to come and see for myself." she shrugged.

Noah believed that he didn't know if he was disappointed by her answer or if he was flattered. He would have been disappointed because he was expecting something deeper. Maybe she was there because she wanted to bond with a group of people that shared her ideologies but she was just here to see who had made a code. He stroked his chin. "How big are your dreams?" He suddenly asked. He crossed his legs and leaned back. This was the main question. The important question. It would determine if she would join in or not. She replied again without missing a beat. "I do not measure the size of dreams. I believe dreams are dreams. My dreams are my dreams and your dreams are your dreams. All dreams are valid."

Noah blinked. He wasn't expecting such an answer. He took a deep breath as a small smile began to grow on his lips. So, she did believe in big dreams, she just wasn't qualifying them. He was half expecting her to say something rehearsed. Her statement made him think deeply. He was so used to people calling him a genius and it made him feel superior to others sometimes. While other people in the community said that they wanted to build a family, build a house and probably raise some chickens and cows, he was here thinking of making robots and taking over the country. So, somehow, he did feel that his dream was bigger. But her statement put things in perspective for him. Maybe, just maybe those people who he thought their dreams were small actually thought their dreams were big to them. They let their imaginations stretch as far as they wanted and it was big enough for them. Also, his dreams were big to him. There was no set standard of measuring them. "I think that is a very interesting answer," he said. She smiled. It was small and respectful like she was addressing it to a boss in an office.

"One last question," he said. All the while Jedidiah was watching them from the kitchen. Noah was well aware of his presence and Noah believed this was a question Jedidiah would have wanted to ask as well. He would have wanted Noah to go straight to the point because it was obvious the girl didn't exactly know what she was there for. Noah admired her guts. She had seen a random flyer from nowhere, decoded the message and she had showed up in front of a stranger's door just because she was curious about who made the message. With every minute that passed and every word that came out of her mouth he thought her to be quite interesting. He felt the need to know more about who she was. Such an odd character. He leaned closer to her like he normally did with his friends but she didn't lean back to him. He had to remind himself that this person was a stranger. He cleared his throat and brought his tone down to a whisper. "Okay so, this is why I put out the flyer. I have a plan and my plan is to create robots. Robots that would keep the society in check. It was a half lie but he wasn't so bent on revealing his reason yet. As they worked together, he would see if she was trustworthy and he would reveal it to her.

She nodded like it was an everyday thing to hear on the streets or in the market. "That is a very interesting dream of yours. So, how do you plan on making those robots then?" He went on to tell her the whole adventure of what they had gone through making the first robot. How the first robot exploded, how they applied for the grant and how they were rejected by the government because they were

Amish. It was odd how she didn't even comment on their dressing. Not once had she looked at them with disdain or malicious intent. She took it in her stride like she had come across normal people. This girl was different from most people. He saw it in the way she moved the way she thought, her ideas and her behavior. She was a radical person she didn't think like the average person and Noah decided she would be a good addition to the group "Congratulations." He stretched out his arm for a handshake. She took it in her palm and firmly shook him.

"Welcome, my name is Noah and the other person standing over there is Jedidiah. Jedidiah waved at her with a small smile. Noah faced Jedidiah. "Do you agree to let her in on our plan?" Jedidiah said, "Yes, I agree. She has a curious mind and she looks like someone who loves adventure. We need people like that on the team." Jedidiah finished saying exactly what Noah had thought. Days passed and they became more familiar with Rachel. She began to brainstorm with them as well. It was hard keeping it a secret from the girls. The time they spent with them became lesser and lesser but Noah had made this decision. He was tired of dragging people along who didn't want to be there with him. He needed people with like mind to push him as well. There was no time to dilly dally. Many times, they would give the girls excuses on why they couldn't come into the room or why they had to go out. On their scouting missions, they looked for scraps as much as possible and they pooled it together in the room. Rachel had said they would need a bigger space but they would have to make do with their room for now. Surprisingly another person showed up to join their group and he fit just perfectly. His name was Ryan.

So, it was like these two people had replaced Anita and Lizzy. Noah loved his friends but he needed this people with him. He went on for a while until their luck finally ran out. Rachel was saying her goodbyes and just as she was leaving the room, Anita opened the door. Everything that happened after was a blur. She had stormed into the room to see so many scrap metals, wires and other things. Lizzie had followed too. The look of betrayal that flashed across their faces made Noah to feel so guilty. He couldn't find the words to say to calm them down. "So, this is what you have been doing?" Anita said. Lizzie said, "I can't believe you guys. So, you don't trust us enough." Noah shook his head. "No, no, I trust you but the both of you give the impression that you are not interested in what I do. I needed to find people with like minds. It is not about you, it is about me." Anita threw her head back. "How stupid do you think we are Noah? What do you actually take us for?"

Lizzie placed her hand on her hips, a frown on her forehead. Even Lizzie was angry. He ran a palm down his face. This was embarrassing. Jedidiah said nothing as well as Rachel. Ryan had gone out for something. They probably didn't even know that they had friends beside them in the other room. This was bad.

Chapter Eleven

Anita walked out slamming the door behind her. This time Lizzy spoke. "Noah, I know you see yourself as genius but do you think that the whole time, we spent following you around was for nothing? We trusted in your abilities and that was why we were with you all the way. Yes, we argued. Yes, we disagreed over some petty things but that doesn't mean you should hide it from us. Is our friendship a joke to you?" Noah could feel the heat coming from Lizzie. She gave Jedidiah a heated glare and walked out. There was silence in the room for some seconds it was thick. So thick you could pass a knife through it. He turned to Rachel. "I'm so sorry about that. There's just some issue between us."

She nodded and raised her arms. "No problem. I'm good. Are you okay?" She looked genuinely worried. He bit his lip and looked elsewhere. "I think I'm okay." He went out to receive some fresh air. The moon was high in the sky and it looked so lonely alone with other stars blinking around it. Why did he think it was lonely? He thought the moon resembled him. The moon was like a big figure and the people that surrounded the moon seemed small. There was a lot of pressure on that big ball of light to perform. That was what made Noah feel pressure to live up to the expectation of being a genius. He stuffed his hands in his pocket and started to stroll down the street. It was much busier than the daytime probably because a lot of people were returning from work and businesses were closing down. He went to the park and laid on the grass counting the stars above him.

It wasn't up to five minutes; a shadow was cast over him. He looked to his side. Rachel stood there observing him. He sighed and continued to stare at the moon letting his thoughts take over. He thought of his friends' words and how he made them feel like their friendship was nothing. It definitely wasn't anything they were there for him throughout the good and the bad times. When his parents died, when everything was horrible, they were there to cheer him up and to share his dreams. Why did he exclude them? Why did he think that they would not be able to handle him. He felt the air shift beside him. Rachel laid on the grass too. "You don't have to be here. Go home, it's late," he said.

Rachel kept mute, ignoring his words. He sighed again. It was very audible and heavy telling of the weight on his chest. Rachel suddenly said, "Really, tell me why you are making robots." He shifted his head to look at her. The moon gleaned on her face reflecting off her skin so it's glowed. While working on the robots, he didn't have the opportunity to really see her but now he saw her real clearly. The curve of her lips, the angles on her face, the slight frown that made her brows to meet in the middle and the sharpness of her nose. Her glasses sat at an odd angle on her face because she was lying on her head. He closed his eyes reliving everything that had happened since they came to the city. He decided to cut it short. Right from day one, Rachel had known something was up. He had really underestimated her when he gave her such a mundane reason.

He spoke. "I want to get a research facility to make robots and release them into the American society because I simply do not like them." Hearing him say it out loud made him chuckle. He was indeed a mad person. He couldn't believe he had come this far just because of that. They had started on the basis of the Rumspringa and it had started with just one robot as a prank. But it had become more. "Do you know why I like the Planet Pluto," he asked. "Pluto is no longer a planet," she declared. "Why do you think so? Because the government says so?" "No, because they have proof." It is considered a dwarf planet. The IAU announced it back in 2006. Noah didn't want to listen to whatever she was going to say about it. He just wanted to air his opinion so he ignored her statement and continued. "I see Pluto as that guy who is separated from the bunch. It is the smallest planet there is among all the planets. How does Pluto feel? Intimidated? Special? Different? Those are examples of how I feel just like Pluto. My mind is too much for a lot of people and I have to stifle myself."

She faced him and said, "Well, I don't think you are odd. You are not odd. You are just different and different is okay sometimes." He also turned to face her. He didn't know if he should believe her words or if he should just snap back to reality. Suddenly a feeling began to grow in his chest. They locked eyes and he kept his gaze on her the specs of gold swirling in her eyes seemed to glimmer under the moonlight. They were just inches away from each other. He had never been so close to a girl before. He took note of the freckles dotting the bridge of her nose. From her eyes, he moved to her nose and then her lips and then looked back up. The distance between them reduced. A part of him wanted to draw back and then the other parts pushed him forward, closer and closer until their noses met. Her gaze was fiery, swelling with something that he couldn't understand, something he had never seen directed at him. He wanted his lips to meet hers. There was tension growing between them. He pushed her neck closer and then met her lips in a soft kiss.

Sparks erupted in his belly he pressed harder on her lips wanting to let the memory being printed in his mind. Her hand pushed his hat off, tangling her fingers with his hair and she deepened the kiss taking his lips in hers. He had never felt like this before. It thrilled him and at the same time it's scared him. Suddenly, as if trying to draw him out of his trance he remembered that he was Amish and he wasn't supposed to be kissing an Englisher outside of marriage. He drew back with a gasp, eyes wide open. What was he doing? He quickly stood on his feet, dusting off the sand on his suspenders. "I'm sorry," he said.

Rachel stood and dusted her jeans. "No, it's alright. I enjoyed it anyway." she shrugged. "I would want to kiss you again but I don't think you are open to it." He felt a rush of heat spread through his cheeks and he looked away. Rachel said, "You're cute." The next day when he was sure the fire had died down a bit, he called his friends together again. "I know I have been really stupid for the past few months and it's becoming a habit of me to apologies over and over again. But I beg you to bear with me. Lizzy, you have been a great friend even if I met you through Anita. You are very supportive of me and my ambitions, you're always there to cheer me and I appreciate it a lot." He turned to Anita. "I would have loved to talk to you in private but I feel it is right that I apologize in front of everybody. I know how much you have invested in me. You are my twin; my other half and I do not take that bond for granted. I only felt I was a burden to the two of you with my ideas and my dreams. We see how we turned out the other day. We fought."

At this, Anita turned the other way. He continued, "And please don't take this out on Jedidiah. I forced him into this. It has nothing to do with him. I was carried away by what I wanted and I didn't consider that it would hurt you to exclude you guys. But it was all in your best interest. I wanted all of us to be satisfied and be happy. Will you forgive me," he said. "I will think about it," Lizzy replied. Anita on the other hand just stood up and left the room while Noah followed after her. She walked briskly but she didn't get far enough before he blocked her way. "Move," she said, glaring daggers at him. "Anita, I'm sorry." "Sorry for yourself." She made to move past him but he grabbed her arms.

"I'm sorry," he said, "I really wanted to tell you but I didn't want you to start trying to change my mind or make me feel like I was doing too much." "Is that why?" she said. An abundance of ugly tears covered her eyes and her voice broke. "So that is why you are tired of me. You want to get rid of me." Noah didn't let her finish he pulled her in for a hug. "You are my sister, my twin. I would never want to get rid of you. I just get annoyed sometimes and I want peace with people who would accept me for me. We are the only ones we've got in this world. Since dad died a year ago." He could feel her tears seep into the fabric of his shirt. He too felt tears burn at the back of his eyes. He pushed back, placed his hands on her shoulders and said, "Let's keep this behind us. Let's look forward to a better future. I'm still pursuing my plan of making the robots. If you want to join me, fine. If you don't, good luck. But, this is my decision and I'm going to follow through with it." Again, like a telepathic connection there was a silent agreement between them.

Things were looking up again but it was obvious they didn't have the funds to create another robot but they had started something. He, Rachel, Jedidiah and Ryan were building something but even then, the quality was too subpar to give any hopeful result. With every day that passed, Noah grew less and less hopeful. There was only so much his recruited hands could do. They needed funds badly. The pastries were going on well but most of the money had gone into paying their rent and stocking up their supplies. At this rate it would take six months before he would finish a robot, but it was getting frustrating. That was until one day, Jedidiah made a suggestion. He asked about the Pell Grant. Anita said she had not checked on it in a while. So, he asked her to. Then she came back and told them that the application was now open.

That was when Jedidiah said what was in his mind. "Let's apply under a fake name," he said. Anita as usual was not open to it but they had come a long way. They had conquered so many obstacles, they had done everything, taken risks and yet they were still standing. So, Noah had every reason to believe that this was what they were meant to do. Pluto was definitely a planet. The government was up to something. It was a hunch and it was something he would not let go of. How could they discard Pluto just like that? After a vote with Anita being the only one who voted against it, they agreed that Lizzy should write the letters but this time under a fake company name. This time they were not the ones who submitted the grant application. They gave it to Rachel to go to the company to submit it. Now they would wait another month. It was a very grueling thirty days. What if it came out negative again? They had tried so many things and Noah was starting to become very cautious of bringing up their hopes again. But fortunately, very fortunately, as they gathered around the computer in

the internet cafe and they opened the email, the saw
in big bold capital letters:

CONGRATULATIONS: You have been awarded a
Pell Grant and a PPP loan.

It was shouts of joy and jubilation after that.

Chapter Twelve

Noah had almost cried when he had seen the
letter. They had received free money so they can
buy a facility. They decided Belle Isle would be a
good place to hide in plan site. many people stop
going there a long time ago. That and it was a lot of
abandoned building they had to choose from to rent.

Plus they though they were near international water because they are between Detroit and Canada. He could not believe his eyes. They screamed so much they had to be chased out of the internet café. There was so much they wanted to say to each other but the wide grins on their faces said it all. They splurged all the money on things as they walked back to the apartment. This was it; this is what they worked for. They had grinded for months, pooling solutions, falling and rising often. They deserved this. In his room, as he lay on his bed, the tears finally fell. This was actually happening and it was all thanks to his friends. For Lizzie's good letter writing, for Jedidiah's idea, for Anita's encouragement. They all together led to this moment. They were just sixteen-year-olds and they had dared the status quo.

While people would think they had gone mad for applying for the government grant for an research facility. his friends crossed the hurdle of unbelief and they pushed and now they had already entered a place of jubilation. Things were finally looking up. That night as they gathered in Noah's room under the moonlight, they cried their eyes out and then they laughed and then they shook each other, then they prayed. This was a new dispensation. They were entering into another dimension of their lives. They would have to move to the Belle Island soon because that was where the research facility was. He hugged each and every one of them telling them how much he loved them. He also thanked Rachel and Ryan for their contribution to their plans.

It wasn't over yet. They would have to go to the company and confirm their Grant acceptance according to the letter. They were going to be interviewed. Already, there was the obstacle of them being Amish. It was then Lizzy had suggested that they finally buy the Englishers clothes which they had been planning to get for long time. The next day, they got set to go to the shopping mall. The clothes with different varieties for the women looked much more fashionable than what he saw for the men. He picked out plain pants and polos while Jedidiah went over the top. Jedidiah picked out shorts, sleeveless polos and black air force ones to go with them. while Noah had decided he would try something that he was more used to. Jedidiah had decided to damn all the consequences. Anita picked simple dresses that were in a different style from what she wore. The dress was much more shorter stopping at her knee and the sleeves were shorter. So, Lizzy picked the same. Unlike the plain dresses they wore, these were decorated with different things like buttons and ribbons. As they tried on the clothes in front of the mirrors, it was obvious that this was actually happening. They were actually going to get a research facility and their lives were on the way to getting a new look. Earlier, Anita had searched what people wore during interviews. She had written it in her note as usual so she asked the attendant where the suit was and a suit skirt.

As expected, they were attracting a lot of attention. They were probably thinking what people like them were doing in such a sophisticated place as the boutique. But months of drawing this kind of attention had shaped them. Noah loved this Rumspringa because, no matter how much people had tried to step on them, they still stood strong and they still stood confident in their identity as Amish people. Finally, the day came for the interview. It had been decided that only Jedidiah and Noah would be going to the building because they were the ones who knew most about the robot plan and how they were going to carry it out. They boarded a taxi to the building. The whole ride was tense. This was a defining moment. If they messed up, it was over for them. They had celebrated and come all the way to this point, they could not afford to go back empty.

The building rose and stretched into the sky, its numerous windows glittering as the sun reflected off them. It took everything in Noah to steady himself as he raised his head and followed the length of the skyscraper. So, this was what they were going to face. He suddenly felt a wave of nerves overwhelm him. They were just sixteen and Amish people. This was something they were not used to. He had never seen the building so tall even though he had read about the skyscrapers in his textbooks. They entered inside into a lobby with golden light fixtures and people milling about in dark suits, holding suitcases. He looked down on his suit. It was okay. It looked like the ones he saw in magazines. But compared to these people, he thought his suit look like rags. Their apparel was sharp and shiny, blacker than his. He steeled himself against the nerves and they went to the reception desk.

"Hello," he said, clearing his throat. He could feel the nerves take over his mind. He quickly cleared his throat and tipped his hat at the lady. She was typing on something and briefly looked up. Then back at her computer. "How can I help you, sir?" "We are here for the grant interview, we have been offered the grant," Noah said. "Okay, so take the elevator to the tenth floor and immediately by your right, you will see an office." Noah had never used an elevator before. He didn't want to show it. He moved away. Not to the elevator, away from the elevator and away from the reception table. He looked to Jedidiah. What he saw was confirmation.

They didn't know how they would use the elevator, what kind of buttons needed to be pressed to go up…

It was better for them to use the stairs instead. If they used the elevator and he got them lost, that would be a problem. So, they use the stairs to climb up ten stories. At the end of it, Noah was a gasping mess. He had done a lot of work at the farm but he had never exerted himself like this before. They sat on the last step of the floor, both of them clutching their chests. This wasn't how they had expected it to go. For the next five minutes, they remained there catching their breath as their heart beat began to steady. True to the receptionist words, by their immediate right there was an office. They knocked on the office door quickly straightening their suits and waited for a reply. "Come in," they heard. Before they moved in, they looked at each other, shook their hands and nodded. It was time to get the bag.

Like morphing in from the Sahara Desert into the North Pole they entered into an office where the temperature was below-zero if Noah could say so himself. He shivered and tightened his coat around his torso. A man sat behind a large desk decked with stacks of paper, a plaque, a laptop and cups filled with pens. He motioned for them to sit down on the large chairs in front of him. When they were settled, he tipped down his glasses on the bridge of his nose and he said, "I received a call from the Secretary that you were given the Grant." They both nodded eagerly. Noah leaned forward. "We are here for the interview."

"Ah, the interview," the man said and took a stack of documents lining them up one by one. He did this for about five minutes and Noah was starting to wonder if he had forgotten that two people were sitting in front of him. He finally looked up. He said, "You can… just don't worry about that." "Huh?" Noah said. What was this man talking about? Was it a test? He tried to understand what he meant by that. He looked to Jedidiah beside him who held the same confused expression. "Yeah, see I don't really want to be doing this right now. I had a bad day today. So, I will just give you the key to the facility and the documents." He had on a smile on his face as he said this. Was he really being serious? Noah exchanged looks with Jedidiah. They couldn't believe this was happening. The man groaned and massaged his forehead, "I really need to leave now. I've got a long day ahead." he stood up. Jedidiah and Noah joined him on their feet as well. He opened his drawer and gave them a small envelope with some documents in a larger brown envelope.

"You can be on your way now I'll be leaving." Noah and Jedidiah left the place dumbstruck. They couldn't believe their luck. They had gotten it on a platter of gold. Information reaching them that, it was about three people who did interviews and they had fortunately been paired with someone who didn't give a hoot about anything. Luck was literally on their side The next couple of days were a blur. They were preparing to move to Belle Isle. There was a certain feeling in the air. A feeling of anticipation and what the future held for them. Their luggage as usual was light but because of their stay in the apartment there were a few other added things. They picked the date to travel with the money they saved from baking and selling their pastries. To his greatest surprise, Rachel offered to come along. He didn't know much about her but he presumed she had a family. He drew her aside to asked her why she would want to come all the way to that place just because of something he envisioned.

Typical Rachel, she shrugged and said "There's no way I'm missing out on something this phenomenal. On the way there they realized that they had to stop calling it the research facility, it sounded strange. But they didn't know what to call it. Everything on short notice sounded it stupid, so research facility it was. Honestly, I thought you were doing a bit too much when you said you would get a research facility but it's happened and I have a feeling that being with you is going to bring me good luck in some way." Noah didn't know what to say to this. He asked her if she was really sure she wanted to do it. After all, he was going to be responsible for her if she came along. He wanted to be sure she really knew what she was doing. Without a second thought she nodded like this was a decision she had been prepared for all her life. Noah would not force her to stay back. He loved when people also tried to explore just like him. He knew what it felt to be asked to stifle his mind and his dream so he let her come along. The day finally came and they all packed their luggage into the truck they had called. When they finished, they gathered in front of the apartment. Jedidiah's aunt had refused to see them but Noah hoped that she knew how grateful they were for letting them use and stay in her apartment. "So, this is it," Lizzy said

Anita came up beside Noah. "We made it so many memories here. I already miss it," she said. Jedidiah sighed and stuffed his hands into his pocket, "We fought a lot, and we were really an unhealthy bunch. But you know what? It made us better." Noah threw his hands over Anita and Jedidiah's necks. "Yeah, it did and I'm happy for every step we have made to be in this moment."

Suddenly, he began to feel emotional. Tears burned at the back of his eyes as the memories flooded his brain like a rushing river. They were moving forward and nothing would come between them." He had a purpose; he had a plan and that was what sat at the front of his mind. He was going to do it: make robots, release them into the American society and make them feel for once what it was like to be harassed like they were. They entered the truck and in the next five minutes they bade goodbye to the apartment and the neighborhood. He would miss this part of his life. Farewell, he thought.

Chapter Thirteen

They finally reached the place. The research facility was set on an island away from most open things around them. The only things they can see from the roof are the light tower and something the locals called the Giant Slide. It was like a large warehouse. When they had arrived, they looked at the building in awe. It was a big Block spanning several kilometers of the land. They couldn't believe their eyes. They had worked for this and they had gotten it. It still sounded so surreal. Noah believed he could achieve his dreams but seeing it in front of him was something else. He got the keys and opened it the door padlocked with a chain. If the outside made them surprised, the inside made them yell in awe. They turned it into a state-of-the-art research facility decked with everything he would need to mass produce the robots. There would be a lab where they tested out things. There were enough materials, metals, wires, motors and everything they needed had already been provided

There were conveyor belts, machines and robot hands that assembled the parts. The plastic needed to shaped the body of the robots into a human looking one was available. He called his friends together and reminded them why they were doing this. Each of them had their own grudges against the Americans since they had been released into the society and each of them was doing this to get back at them. To teach them a lesson that the Amish people were not to be played with. Production began. All hands were on deck. Noah and Jedidiah worked on the designs while Lizzy, Anita and Rachel worked in the production areas. He was doing this because the Americans had insulted him and stepped all over him and his friends. Also, he was going to get back at the government.

They thought they could lie about something as important as a planet. He would give them something else to focus on definitely. So, the days passed into weeks. The production went swiftly. They were a team and they worked well together. There was a house just beside the research facility, so they lived there close to the building. One day, suddenly there was news of a market crash. This affected them badly because the stock market was crashing and a lot of people were withdrawing their investments in companies. Even the Grant company had informed them that they might withdraw their support of the facility. This was bad. They had come so far. The production was almost finished, why was this happening now?

They had gathered in the small meeting room that they chose. Finally, they had upgraded from Noah's room to an official meeting room. But that was the least of his problems. He paced and bit his lips. "What are we going to do?" he asked. Rachel was the one who spoke. "If they eventually withdraw their support, the research facility would have to shut down because obviously we don't have any money." she let out a bitter laugh but she continued, "I have an idea. We could apply for loans. PPP loans and use it to complete the robot production." Since the others didn't have anything to say to contribute, they decided to go with what Rachel suggested. Noah once again was grateful for the people he had surrounding him he couldn't have come this far without them and their ideas. So many times he had found himself stuck between the devil and the deep blue sea but they managed to pull him out. It was this plan they followed while the companies began to crash because stock market investors pulled out. They decided to apply for loans. With their research facility and the promise of what they were building it was easier to get loans because who else in the whole of the country had a research facility dedicated to creating robots for environmental and climate change issues.

They opened separate bank accounts to hold these loans and used them to fund the rest of the production. Things were going fine. He had given himself a timeline and they were nearing the end of this timeline. If only Noah knew that they were being watched. And it wasn't just being watched, it was who was watching them. They had been working on another batch of robots when a man presented himself at the entrance of the warehouse. This was the first time they had someone else who wasn't part of the team come to the Research facility. Instantly their alarm signals were heightened. Noah took off his lab coat and approached the man at the entrance. The man had a scary look to him. He was donned in a black pressed suit with black sunglasses that gleamed under the sunlight and a coyly device stretched over his ears. He held a suitcase by his side and everything about him reminded Noah of a spy. As he approached, the man stuffed his fingers into his breast pocket and pulled out a card. He spoke, his voice was stiff and robot-like. "I am agent Mark," he said putting his card in front of their faces.

They looked at the card. Noah heard Anita gasp beside him. Something was wrong. He read the details. There was a name and then the logo which said FBI. Agent Coulson withdrew his card and said, I've been sent here to inspect the facility. You will do well to let me do my job," he declared. Noah felt his heart trip in his chest. He had not had this feeling in a long time. Everything was going well. Why were they suddenly asking to search the facility? They were new to this. They didn't know what to say, even Rachel had backed down. They let him through. He inspected the place and while he did, he took notes. Noah itched to know what the notes were about. "So, you make robot here," the agent asked

Noah fell into step beside him. "Yes, we do." "And what are these robots supposed to be for?" "Well, we are creating them to check environmental issues and climate change." Agent Coulson stopped and then he turned to Noah, studied him from his head to his two and then shifted his gaze to the ones behind him. "So…" he drawled, "What exactly do these robots do to fight climate change?" Noah felt a lump grow in his throat. He swallowed and looked at his friends. Maybe for help or for encouragement, he wasn't sure but he had never thought of this question. Nobody had bothered to ask it. Jedidiah step forward. "I'm afraid that is confidential information. We cannot divulge that at the moment until we are ready to release the robots." Agent Coulson looked at Jedidiah for longer than was usual. His glasses were covering his eyes so they weren't able to see the expression on his face and understand what he was thinking. But finally, he nodded and said, "Okay then, can I see your IDs? This is an order from the FBI." Anita stepped forward on impulse. "Well, we do not have our IDs here at the moment. I'm afraid you would have to wait for us to go get it."

Noah raised his brows. Get the ID from where? What was Anita thinking? Where were they going to get IDs from? The thought had never crossed his mind that they were supposed to get IDs. Everything was going fine and nobody thought to think of what kind of obstacles they would have faced as they worked on production. Agent Coulson nodded and wrote something in his note. He said, "I am done here for the day. We will report back to you soon." There was a way he said it that made a shiver run down Noah's spine. What did he mean by that? Immediately, he asked them to gather at the meeting room. "What did he mean by he would be back?" Lizzy said. "I don't know, I don't know." Noah was pacing around the room. "I think trouble is coming. We have to increase production of our robot by fifty percent at least."

Jedidiah said, "Isn't that going to stress the machines?" Noah replied, "I don't think so. We can increase the efficiency of the machines if we want to. We have only been going at a slower pace because there was no need to go at a faster pace. Do you understand?" Anita nodded and the rest nodded too. So, they set to work. The air in the facility had changed. There was an urgency that needed to be fulfilled. Noah was at the top of his toes and he kept everybody on their toes to. They worked overtime, overnight and they slept little. They had to complete it before any trouble came. He thought of his parents and his home back at the community. It had been so long since he saw them. He knew they would be wondering where they were and what they were doing at that moment or what they had made their lives to turn out to. He also knew there was the big question on their mind if they would decide to stay with the modern society or if he would return to the Amish community. He didn't know yet. Just like how he had been all his life, half of him loved his community and the other half loved what the modern society had to offer.

In the midst of all the chaos and everything that was happening, he took out time alone and drafted a long letter to his family telling them how things had been going with them. He started from the beginning. Everything they had done how their rumspringa had turned out for them, how they had fought and how they had stood tall in the midst of horrible glares and malicious stares. He told him of how he had met a girl who he seemed to like. He told them how he had fought with Anita over their differences and how they had reconciled. He told them how they had caused a blackout in the apartment. He wanted to be as transparent as possible. There was no need to hide. Everybody knew what the Rumspringa entailed and he was going to be as open as possible. He wanted them to trust him. He knew that most of the contents of the letter would set them off because he had done so many things that were against there are rules. But again, it was the rumspringa and it was allowed. So, nobody could fault him for his deeds. He just wanted to make sure they knew he was okay and there was a scary part of him that informed him that he was doing this just in case things went south.

What if you never got to see them again? He shuddered at the thought. He shouldn't be thinking like that. He should be the one encouraging his friends. He was somewhat the leader of the group and he knew that they also had their fears. So, he had to stay strong and stay firm. When he was done with the letter, he went out and sent it to the post office to be sent to the Amish community. They had told him it would take at least four days for the letter to arrive. He hoped by then, things would be normal. Or so he thought. Because why was it that on the very next day after the agent had arrived, five police cars pulled up in front of the warehouse. They were almost through with the production. They heard the sirens first. It was a whoop that reminded him of blaring alarms. Noah stopped what he was doing took off his gloves and his goggles and then looked outside the window. There, five police cars pulled up in front of the warehouse. His mouth dropped open. He rushed down to meet the others also wearing shocked looks. A man in a police uniform came out holding a megaphone.

It clicked and his voice blasted through. "You are under arrest for forgery and infringement on government property." Noah looked at Rachel to see if she could understand what they were saying. What do they mean by infringement on government property? They had been given the grant fair and square. Clutched his arm in tears. The fear that struck her face made him shiver. If anybody had to go out there, it should be him. So, he looked at them, faced them, his friends, his allies and his companions. The looks on their faces tore through his chest and he wanted to retch his heart out the way it squeezed painfully inside. There were a lot of thoughts crashing through his mind. He was confused, he was scared and he was perplexed. Not wanting to give off a scared aura, he stood and set his face in a straight expression and then called Jedidiah aside.

"Jedidiah, I need you to do something for me. Do not tell the others. I need you to set the robot to be released right now." Jedidiah paused and gave him an incredulous look. "Right now?" "Yes, right now," Noah said. "I know that we have not finished and I know that there are still a lot of modifications we need to do. But I think it is ready enough to be tested. Release the robots right now in the next five minutes. Set a timer." Noah didn't wait for him to confirm. He left Jedidiah and then went to the girls. "Don't worry, just stay here. I'm going to take care of it." With one step in front of the other, he approached the entrance, his hands raised to show that he was not holding any weapon and he did not mean any harm. "You are under arrest," the policeman said. Noah knew that. He understood that part. "For what?" he asked. "You applied for the Pell grant and forged your identity, lying about the company that you were running. Yes or no?"

Noah couldn't find his voice. He faltered and looked elsewhere. "You are also under arrest for planning to take over the American government." Noah clenched his hands into fists. How did they know that. He had only told his friends. That was when the man looked behind him and said, "Thank you, agent Rachel." Noah didn't think he heard properly. His bones froze and his blood simmered under his skin. Slowly, he turned around to see who was being referred to as an agent. Lo and behold, it was the Rachel he had brought into his team and the one he had kissed under the moonlight that day. He couldn't believe his eyes. He could feel tears spring up behind his eyeballs and he blinked them away. No wonder she was hell-bent on going with them to the island. He had found it suspicious at first but he had thought that she was just as interested as he was in making the robots.

Betrayal was evident in his expression. He gritted his teeth and then looked back at the policeman. Even if Noah was going to cry, it would not be in front of her." He couldn't believe he trusted her. That he had taken her as a friend too and he had even started to have feelings for her. He almost laughed at the absurdity of it all. "So, what are you going to do with us?" he asked. That was the most important question. What would they do with him and his friends. Would they have to go to prison? The thought made his heart clench harder. It was doing that a lot lately and if care was not taken, he would fall into a heart attack. The sirens were still blaring, the lights turned and turned, the police officers that stood in front of him were holding guns in his direction and his friends were behind in the warehouse. He could feel the weight of everything rest on his shoulders. He just wanted to collapse and let the earth swallow him.

All the while he thought he had found a friend in Rachel but she had stabbed him in the back. In fact, from the very first day, she was never there for them she was there as an agent. He turned to her, "When did this start?" he asked. "Was it the first day you came?" Rachel walked over to the policeman, a swagger in her steps. She resumed position beside them, "of course I came there because I was an agent. Do you think I would risk myself to just go anywhere for the sake of some random flyer?" Noah beat back a curse. He couldn't believe his ears. "So, everything we shared was nothing to you." She shrugged. "I admit that I was taken away by your way of thinking. But at the same time, come on, you want to create robots to invade American society. I mean listen to yourself? Do you not think that is going overboard?"

"No, I don't." Noah began to relive the memories that he had experienced. "If only you people had accepted us for who we are and left us to ourselves, we would not be having this conversation today. And that lie about Pluto not being a planet, what's that about? Your history is filled with so much missing pages and so many things that make people fear. I do not want a part of it. We didn't want a part of it but you guys still went out of your way to make us feel inferior and step all over us. This is just my own way of revenge." By the end of the speech, he could feel anger bubble in his heart and the blood under his skin simmered. Not only did day step all over them they had sent somebody to betray them. He was done. In the next second, he turned behind him and yelled, "Jedidiah now!"

"Don't move!" the police men were coming closer to him. "I'm not moving," he said sending them a smirk. Soon, this will be over. Hopefully. Immediately, there was a siren coming from the warehouse. It pierced through the air like an alarm signal. The police were disoriented for a second. They look towards the warehouse and they looked at him. "What have you done?" Noah only smiled. Immediately, from nowhere, droves and droves of robots began to pour from the Doors His robots were currently ready. But for some reason he had only shared this information with Jedidiah and he made the others to work continuously on the robots. But he had programmed them enough to be released already. Just in case there was an emergency. He had created a program that made them recognize their faces and yes, that was including Rachel. So, they weren't going to attack her. But the appearance of the hundreds of robots pouring out from the doors was enough to set them off.

Noah took the destruction in his stride and ran back to the warehouse. The robots advanced towards the policemen. The first robot that came in front of them policeman who was nearer, grabbed the man by his shirt and flung him a distance away. Noah smiled to himself. Yes, it was a success. His robot had done exactly as he had planned. "Quick, we need to escape," he said once he entered into the place. Jedidiah and Lizzy were quick on their feet. Anita on the other hand, she stood, frozen on the spot. Noah grabbed her arm and pulled her along, snapping her from her trance. He wasn't really expecting something like this to happen in a million years, but he had made preparations just in case.

"Go through the back," he commanded watching them run forward.

Anita stopped. "Aren't you coming?"

"Go, I have something to take care of," he said.

She hesitated.

"Just go, Anita. I promise, I'm right behind you." She nodded and followed after the others. Noah hoped they would find their way out and get to safety. With the grant, he had bought a small vehicle. Whenever they needed to go to town, they used it to go through the small strip of land connecting the island to the town. But, there was a catch. It was Rachel who drove. Now, she was an enemy. Jedidiah had mentioned that his brother had secretly thought him how to drive. So, he was banking on that. Noah rushed up the stairs into the control room. He could hear the screams outside. Still, he needed to be quick. He pressed some buttons. "Self-destruct activated. Count down in ten seconds." Immediately he rushed downstairs and found them already stuffed in the car. He joined them. Jedidiah did a sign of the cross, started the engine and drove. It was a bumpy ride but they escaped through the land. Once ten seconds passed. There was a massive bang behind them.

They all looked back to see the research facility, exploding. Everything scattering and coming to nothing. They had no IDs, and they lived in a hidden community. So, they were safe. Noah had programmed each robot to fly to different destination and be typical Karen's. For the next couple of days, the headlines were all about the robots. They all cheered and celebrated this achievement. Certainly, their Rumspringa was the best. And the four of them would definitely have a story to tell their grandchildren.